Returning to Peace

Nicole Bodnaresk

First Edition – July 2010

Edited by Ryan Steedman.

ISBN
978-1-77067-086-0 (Hardcover)
978-1-77067-087-7(Paperback)
978-1-77067-088-4 (eBook)

∞

∞

Published by:

Suite 300 – 777 Fort Street
Victoria, BC, Canada V8W 1G9
www.friesenpress.com

For information on bulk orders contact:
info@friesenpress.com or fax 1-888-376-7026

Distributed to the trade by The Ingram Book Company

"... My heart is Venice... a place of beauty, yet filled with melancholy and sadness. Like the cracks on the walls and the water lapping at its doorsteps; it is left. It is not to be fixed because the inevitable will happen. Leave it to follow its natural course. And surely as it goes so will my heart... Too much beauty to do anything about it."

Heavy Eyelids, Cold Tea

Chapter One

A soft aura surrounded the little boy I knew so well as he played in the piazza. If only he knew. His eyes would ever so often dart back to mine and he would smile. Eyes that haunted me overlapped in his, the eyes that I vividly remember as his mothers.

Her heart was in the right place when she first came, though not her mind. As her plane landed at the Marco Polo airport a soft scent infused the air, just as the thousands of other people who have left something behind she too would have the chance.

She carried her physical evidence with a grace and understanding of a woman twice her age. However, she also carried the emotional evidence, something she tries to leave behind. A plane ride away to catch up with her soul. A nervous mind yet a peaceful heart landed two minutes before its due time. There she sat exactly where her soul needed to be. Her thoughts just didn't know it yet...

Jens eyes glaze slowly across her messy handwriting imprinted on the note she had been trying to write for the last two hours, and shrugged. She shrugged because she had accomplished nothing, not because she didn't care. Along with where she sat and her failure to concentrate, she was at a loss for words. Even the thought of this note made her hands develop into a cold and sweaty manner. Her sweaty hands took hold of her thoughts, just for a moment; *what is this all for?* Nevertheless, in spite of everything, let the thought pass with a blink. The life of the note was short lived, with rips and doodles around the edges. Jen couldn't help but wonder exactly how old the paper was, how many days, hours, perhaps even years, how long had it been a part of this world.

This world. As the years past this world became more foreign to her; she was left with more questions then answers. More than ever, the idea of life confused her. Cheers to her father whom doesn't even know she is gone, cheers to her mother whom she never knew, and cheers to Jerry the supposed love of her life. Drinking away her pain with no cup in hand, nothing but a pen, nothing but a hope. An obligation of survival and lack of innocence was how she developed throughout the years.

" Il vostro te, mancanza." A young Italian woman placed a cup of tea in front of her. Breaking Jen from the so-called concentration, she needed to write. Not knowing the language at all, she just nodded her head in acknowledgement and appreciation. Disappointedly, Jen was more like an overwhelmed tourist and caught on only to a few words. Such a beautiful language. A language that appreciates the form of the mouth, lips and tongue. If only Jen knew how to be the language, she could belong. No one would share a second glance at her and question her life.

Her mind continuously questioned her sanity. Leaving her with no answers this became an obsession, which made her second guess her very well being. Jen always acted on impulse; sometimes this got her in more trouble than any good. Therefore, when she found out she was with child the first idea that came to her mind she acted upon.

Before Jen had left, she told no soul of her condition; not her best friend, not her family, not even Jerry. This hopeless note, Jen crumpled and put away. Jerry needs to know, he had the right to know that he is going to be a father in only a months' time. She never thought that her first time would be under her deck on a bed of rocks, but it was.

Her mind wasn't in the right mode, the right frame of mind to write, to hope. The two of them suffered a kind of falling out. Jen couldn't give any more of herself, and Jerry didn't understand. Maybe if she had talked to him, he would have understood, maybe not. This is where she was in her life. In Italy, alone and with child, with no rhyme or reason to her way of life.

Jen's tea was getting cold, so she put away the note, and relax, something well deserved. A strong word perhaps. In Jens mind, she did not deserve to relax, but she needed it. She folded it carefully and placed it in her oversized bag now thinned out as she left most of her possessions at the hotel room. A few clothes she bought before she left with essential cleaning supplies preoccupied the hotel room. Her purse held only a bit of money, an English-Italian translation book, her drivers license, and a picture of Jerry sitting by a lake with the Rocky Mountains in the back ground. He wrote on the back and signed 'with love always.' Everything important to her she hid away in a safe at the bank the first day she arrived. Her passport, some extra money for a return trip and anything she was afraid to lose were taken care of, adding to her extra sense of security.

Jen sipped on the tea and thought it odd that it tasted better cold than it did warm. Perhaps the hot moist day had something to do with it. *Venice is beautiful,* she thought smiling with satisfaction, content with her decision. The café she sat at was just off the Rialto Bridge that crossed over the Grand Canal, at this time of the day polluted with tourists in awe with the city. Often she heard disturbances to the water by a paddle separating and swishing it about. The paddle would then ever so gently tap against the wooden gondola and continue in the same motion prior. She watched as a gondola passed under the bridge, the tourists relaxing, smiling in contentment made her wonder if she would feel the same gliding over the water. More often than not, a small motorboat would be heard from afar. Faint at first, but slowly pushed louder and louder to the ear as it passed underneath the bridge. The gondolas used to be the only way of transportation through the canals as the larger boats stayed on the outskirts of the city, but now it was only kept alive through the romantic ideals that Venice offered. Taxi boats, Vaporettos (water buses) and private boats filled the water these days bringing Jen to reality. However, nothing could break the pure sound of a single instrument, the classical guitar. It enchanted the air with waves of life, beauty, and an untold sorrow. Possibly for the lovers, or the people that wanted to keep the hope alive, Romance de Amour. The music sank into Jen and she knew that it could hypnotize her with a heavy burden, passion. At that moment, there was an anomalous feeling of true innocence held within this instrument. The sound of each note plucked on the guitar flowed as softly as the wind that caressed Jen's face. The precise position of the music was unknown as it bounced across walls and floated along the canal. In the air lingered not only the sound of the stringed instrument, but the smells of Italian cooking. Something, that when thought about, made Jens mouth water, and forced her to recall when her last meal was and if she was due for another one. The vision that surrounded her and the feeling of a life that grew inside her blended into a wondrous picture of perfection.

Venice literally means 'the city of canals' but is also known as the world's theatre. An experienced city that has seen centuries of beauty and terror. Matured by years shown on the faces of buildings but made the city more phenomenal and comforting. A place of romance and a gift for understanding life drifted through the city and absorbed into its creation. Jen could sense it there but could not grasp it, and felt as though it teased her.

Jen finished her tea slowly and spent most of her day in leisure - a foreign feeling to her. She thought that by traveling across the world and filling her senses with new tastes, smells, sights, sounds, and textures she would leave her thoughts behind. She had more time to freely allow her thoughts and emotions to roam over and possess her. She had been in Venice for four days and she spent most of her time lost in her mind, recalling what she left behind and wondering what was in store for her future. She spent her time getting lost weaving on and off the main tourist paths. Never knowing where she was and never looking too hard to find herself.

She tried distracting herself with the little shops by the Piazza San Marco or just off the only bridge over the Grand Canal at the Pte. di Rialto. Never buying anything only looking at the beautiful glass objects made on the island of Murano or the papier-mâché mascherines that stared back at her without eyes. As she wondered away from the Rialto, it felt as though she followed the music. And every time she would see someone come from one of the narrow streets she would look and see if it was herself, and sadly divert her eyes when she realized that it wasn't her. Jen thought that, just, perhaps there might be a chance she could find herself. Silly as it might have sounded it wasn't too much to ask, or so she thought.

These four days did nothing for her grasp of the language and it only frustrated her trying to learn. Every time Jen tried to study her translation book, she would end up throwing it to the other side of her small hotel room. It probably didn't help that she was pregnant, which meant for some pretty nasty mood swings. The mood swings were playing a toll on her, and because she had no one to take them out on, she spent most of her time conjuring up different endings to her story, none of them good. It seemed that only the moments she lost control of her thoughts she could feel joy in small things, such as simply relaxing with tea or wandering around at her own speed.

Peaceful thoughts dissolved as quickly as they arrived. Two days prior Jen threw a delicate teacup to the floor at this cute little restaurant because she could not, for the life of her, understand a single word her waiter said. Feelings overtook her and she acted without thinking about the real world around her. Since than she hadn't been in a 20-foot radius of the place. She had embarrassed herself, and was more than aware of that. The restaurant had no need to question her. No one wanted to get in the way of a pregnant woman. As Jen left the waiter went out of his way to say, 'have a nice day' in a shaky English. Oddly enough bringing her to tears. Jen still had a month left of bizarre moods and changes in her body. One month. She had one month to prepare herself, to figure herself out, go home, and face facts, and to feel what it is like to be a mother. She needed to prepare herself physically and mentally, when she tried, she felt overwhelmed and scared, a feeling she had a hard time going back to. Everything was foreign to her, and although most of it (in fact, all of it) she had brought upon herself, she still felt as though she was in a constant state of uncertainty. It was the least expected place where she felt the most foreign, it was in her own body. Even as she touched her own skin, she felt lost. Hands that didn't belong, skin too white, heavy eyelids, usually light. Jerry's hand slipping away. Possible hope in the form of a little bundle, soon to come.

Just before Jen and Jerry no long existed, they barely shared the odd word, and when they did talk, it was Jerry saying he had enough of Jen's 'sporadic mood changes.' Both drifted apart. Jen knew that she had the power to change the inevitable but she couldn't. Maybe if she told him, he would do the right thing and marry her, take care of her. Dilemmas, however, got the best of her normally straight honest self. She knew she needed to tell him, but the moment had to be right. Little did she know at the time, that this moment would never come.

It really starts six days after the particular moment at the café, ten days in total. Venice already played a toll on Jen's finances. Changed. Ten fucking days, her whole life! At the point of her arrival, she found a nice cozy hotel in the San Marco district, never thinking to look for anything cheaper. Living added up. Venice is not a cheap place to stay, but something drew her to its mystery. This little venture of hers was going to end. Her support and lifeline were dissipating. Concerned yet not concerned enough. The little money she did have would get her a one-way ticket back home from the Marco Polo and hopefully a taxi to her front steps. What did she want to prove to herself? The thought of going home made Jen nervous, which made her scared and put her in a rather bad mood. This day happened to be the day she went into labour.

Angelo was stirred awake by the engines of the vaporetto. Finally, it was ready to move again. It seemed as though the vaporetto had been stopped forever. That, however, was just a malfunction of Angelo's mind and its ability to relate to time. He had spent the majority of his day at Ravenna, a bus ride down the cost of the Adriatic Sea; then went to visit a friend in Burano and was now on his way back to Venice. Aside from the seat he occupied and the two workers of the vaporetto, it was vacant of people. Instead of paying attention to the normal hum of voices, he was forced to listen to the sound of the creaking metal and the water hitting hard against the boat's side.

Although necessity dictated he must stay awake and aware his thoughts drifted into incoherence. It felt good being able to get everything over with. He no longer had to deal with the lawyers or the will, it was finished. He smiled and sighed in relief as he rested his head against the cool window, now fogged with condensation. The lights from Punta Sabboni smeared as Angelo wiped his hand across the window. The vaporetto slowed, its engines swelled and banged into the rubber dock which could be felt as it rumbled across the boat's body. A familiar feeling to the people of Venice. He watched one of the operators tie a rope to the horn on the stop and open the security bar to let people on. Tonight no one was willing to give up the certainty of solid ground. Angelo smiled and laughed to himself, no one had come to disrupt the delicate balance of his universe.

Angelo lived in his last painting. The sun had just started to fade behind the hilly terrain of the beautiful vineyard, almost perfect in vision. The colors flowed together with an unrealistic view of the world. The sun was unseen but it reflected off the leaves of the trees and the blades of grass. Angelo could feel the heat from the sun even though it could not be seen. Softly it caressed his face. There is nothing like an Italian sunset, burning with hot reds and pinks, Reflecting off the water, blues and greens soften and enrich the vision. A peaceful aroma filled his senses as he made his way deeper and deeper into the life of his painting. He needs this serenity more than he realizes. He sleeps cradled by the vaporetto, living in another moment.

He was jolted out of his universe and the vaporetto unexpectedly stopped. On any other night he would have ignored the slam- it was nothing out of the normal- but something told him to wake up.

He slowly straightened up, looking around at all the seats. Still empty. Only the traces of humans existence remained: empty wrappers, muddy footsteps and a scarf left on the back seat. He sat forward on his seat and embraced the one in front looking to the front of the vaporetto. The two doors were closed which made Angelo wonder why he would close them on such a warm night. Force of habit.

Before he could see anything, he heard the faint sound of a feminine voice flowing softly into the interior of the vaporetto. Angelo held his breath to hear what was happening. The stranger's voice soothed into his skin, and created a blanket around him. This voice became familiar, which intrigued him. He moved his head over, back and forth, to try and get a glimpse of her through the glass, but only faintly through the condensation could he see the vaporetto worker. Although he could only hear mumbles, he made out that the female voice was that of a foreigner. The worker was beginning to raise his voice, as if it would help her understand him. Angelo laughed quietly; this had not been the first time he had seen this being done. A natural human tendency. He heard the worker try to speak English to help her, but his accent was so thick and words slurred that it was unintelligible. After a moment went by and the boat was still stopped, Angelo took the initiative to help. English was second nature to him, he had been taught well. He had spent two years of his studies in England to try his hand at acting. At this time in his life Angelo could be described in two words: a 'Young Bohemian.' He lived his life, for the arts. The art of paint, of theatre, of language, of music and the art of love. In Italian, the word for love is Amore. A word most the of world craved for with a secret passion. However in Italia there is no secret with amore; it is the driving force.

By the time Angelo had made it through the doors and to the front, the young woman had stepped on and was trying to keep her balance.

Jen had always been a beautiful girl, and, even now that she was with child, her beauty radiated as though the sun had shifted and set rays of light shooting through a window. She shifted smoothly to the woman that she now was. The aura that surrounded her made her look like a goddess, soft and glazed. Moreover, this particular day she wore her long wavy hair down and an oversized sundress which ever so often slipped from her shoulder, and elongated her neck. Her eyes, uncovered, sparkled in the bright sunlight and her lips, glossed, demanded attention. What was really catching about her was her confidence. She stood that day beyond the point of exhaustion, yet her body was still too proud to show it. The whole day she had been in a fix about what to do with her situation and finally decided to take a walk.

It was hard to fit into the tempo of Italian life. Venice belonged to no one, yet everyone belonged to her. Jen thought that it was Venice changing its rhythm constantly, never realizing that it was, in fact, herself trying to belong.

With it's worn paths and hectic pace at San Zaccaria, Jen boarded the 82 to Lido to spend her day away from the beautiful markets, wonderful little kiosks, and the bundles of people. She tried to get away from the hum of voices so that she could hear her own. But this idea failed. Tanned bodies were everywhere, strewn across the sand outnumbered only slightly by the shells that outlined the push of the waves. Lido was different then Jen had thought it would be, and although it recognizably held a hint of Venice in it, the island had its own demeanor. Lido was filled with cars and buses; oddly enough it made her think of home.

Jen wandered around for most of her day. Only her newfound comfort differentiated today from the days that preceded it. It felt slower here, even though as she walked along the streets the cars zoomed by. Nevertheless, the people came here to relax on the beach; they came here to leave their lives behind if only for a few hours. The island was much larger than Jen had thought. She spent most of her day heading south down the Island, drinking in the sight of the Mediterranean Sea, as it disappeared over the horizon.

Finally, she decided to stop at a more remote area of the beach, here there were a few rocks that she could lean on. Every now and then, someone would walk by and quickly glance in her direction. Jen could not help but wonder what people thought when they walked past her, but didn't dwell on the thought for too long.

Slowly her rapid thoughts were washed away with the falling of the tide. The sound of the waves cradled her to sleep. The world around her morphed into a perfect painting of a sun that had just disappeared from the horizon but left evidence of its beauty upon the rolling hills. Jen had never been there before but in her dreams - a place that would probably never exist.

Bursts of pain shot through her abdomen waking her up with a start. She woke up holding her stomach, it must have been her protective nature to the child that would be. Looking around, not able to remember where she was, she no longer felt the warm sun against her face. Now the sun slept and the day was forever gone. Instant panic ran through her body and pains swelled up. The little bundle inside her was unsatisfied. She had not even recalled falling asleep, and now hours later she would have to pay.

It was a clear evening and the air felt fresh upon Jen's skin, chilling her only slightly. The sea brushed up close to the rocks that cradled her, and the smell of the sea made her feel as if somehow, somewhere, she had just washed up onto shore. Jen wanted to stay, but time was lost to her and she knew she needed to get back to the hotel. As she retraced her footsteps from earlier in the day, it felt as though she had crossed into a different world. Nothing moved. No cars, no people. Even the sound of the wind or the close swaying of the ocean could not be heard. Still. This eerie feeling forced Jen to walk faster. Every now and then feeling a slight pain of resistance from within. It felt as though she was not moving, running on a treadmill, having to work harder than normal to even move.

Is this real? She kept thinking, pinching herself discreetly, walking as fast as she could. Jen was unsure as to how long it took her to get to the vaporetto stop, but it felt like an eternity. As she crossed the street to the stop, she noticed that the vaporetto was leaving. She was forced to a run, which looked more like a hop, screaming, 'Excusi, excusi.' The worker spotted her and yelled something to the driver that made the vaporetto slam into reverse.

The engine screeched making the vehicle stop. Jen moved to the edge of the platform and waited nervously. Please speak English, she thought. Jen was in too much pain to try to concentrate on how to pronounce what she needed to say in Italian. Her hopes were dashed when she tried to speak in English and he only replied in Italian. What was he saying?

The pain in her abdomen increased, causing her to cringe. This stress was too much for her, but she brought it upon herself. In some odd way, she enjoyed the fascination of it all. She only wished that she had someone to share it with. Her mind flashed back to Jerry. She could see him helping her onto the boat. Both of them would be sitting at the back, just because that was their favorite spot and Jerry would have one arm around her shoulder and his other hand resting on her belly. Her daydreams were broken as the Italian man spoke louder. Shaking her head to indicate she didn't understand had no effect. Wasn't that a universal language? She felt like walking away, back to her spot on the beach.

Jen glanced over to an oncoming figure, the way he approached almost made her forget all her problems. His figure was tall and alluring, broad unlike most of the men she had seen around. He stood straight and walked in long strides, confident and with urgency. Jen couldn't help but wonder if she was taking up too much of this passenger's time. He was fashioned with black dress trousers and a shirt with the sleeves rolled up and the collar undone, wrinkled from the wear and tear of the day. Jen imagined him at the beginning of his day with his clothing pressed and freshly shaven, but thought this must suit his style of life more accurately. His short hair looked as though he had just spent the last hour running his hands through it to get that pristine, messy look. His strong jaw line covered in speckles of hair. *Have I seen you before?* Was all she wanted to ask him. As he reached closer, what drew her to this stranger were his haunting eyes. She wasn't sure whether to meet his gaze. *Is it rude in this culture, am I being too bold?* However, she lacked the ability to avert her eyes, so did he.

'Can I help, is right?' He repeated again a little louder. She realized then that she had been holding her breath.

'Yes...' she paused, 'I... you see...' glancing over at the worker, 'I lost track of time and need to find my hotel room.' Without having to ask the stranger, he translated what she said into Italian for the bus driver, who nodded. 'I was wondering if I could get a ride back to Venice. Is this boat going back there?' She went into her purse and held out some money. As the stranger translated for her, the vaporetto worker took her money and nodded repeating 'sit, sit.' He reached into his pouch and brought out a fresh ticket and punched a hole through it, then handed it to Jen.

Jen nodded in thanks, as she walked further to the inside compartment to sit down. The stranger followed behind and sat in the seat opposite her. After an awkward pause, Jen spoke. 'Thank you.' She blushed, her proud manner trying to get in the way, she faced forward not looking into his eyes again. She was drawn to them, but nerves took over.

'You're welcome.' He smiled. This young woman was something else. She looks like a goddess, he thought. Her hair blew in the wind from the open windows and doors. Her lips partially separated were full and tempting. He swallowed hard. Although she wore a dress four times too large, it did not hide her femininity. It clung to her curves, slipping off her shoulder. *A work of art.* He looked at her belly and smiled. She was the most beautiful pregnant woman he had ever laid his eyes upon. *Where was her man?* Angelo thought. *Why is she wandering by herself?* These questions he longed to ask her, but he knew it was not his place.

'Do you like it here?' Angelo asked, trying hard to keep the conversation going. He wanted to protect her, to keep her with him. He knew that as soon as she left the vaporetto he would never see her again, 'It is beautiful, si?' When she didn't answer or even acknowledge his questions he turned to look at her more closely. She was clutching her belly, her hands white.

'Madam, are you feeling alright?' His concern for her was overwhelming, though he had no idea who this woman was. Yet, looking into her eyes, he knew she was genuine. Angelo had never been wrong about anyone before, and she was real.

'Oh yeah... just a bit of a stomach ache... that's all.' She smiled weakly, trying to hide her blood shot eyes. Look away, just look outside.

'Sorry to ask such a delicate question, but how long have you...?' He broke off, as she understood what he was trying to say.

'Oh, no its...' she pats her belly,'... too soon.' Her pains morphed into fears. Jen's body, her baby, had been trying to tell her all day, but she had ignored it. *This doesn't feel right. I don't feel right. Don't be afraid.*

'Well...do not worry. We can get you to a hospital, it will be alright.' *What can I do? Don't panic, keep calm, calm. Console her.*

'Oh, I, I'm waiting until I get home.' She said it as though she actually believed it, laughing ridiculously. 'Its just that, I can't afford...' She stopped, her water was breaking. *Stop, oh please stop.* This was all happening so fast for her, far from the way it was supposed to. She looked over to the stranger, almost embarrassed. He looks too concerned, it's okay, stop breathing hard.

'It seems as though I wet myself.' Jen laughed trying to make the situation lighter. Shut up, don't be stupid. That didn't work; she put her foot in her mouth. Unsuccessful with her attempt, the laughter seemed to flow uncontrollably. She could no longer tell if she was laughing because of what she said or because of the pain.

'Listen, it will be good, right?' Angelo spoke putting his arm on her shoulder. He bundled up his suit coat that he had left on the seat. Oh God, stay calm. I wish I could do more, oh God... 'You should lie across the seat, use this as a pillow.' He spoke as he helped her get into a comfortable position and placed the suit jacket under her head. Just as he was about to move his hands away, Jen caught his right hand. She didn't have to say anything, he understood; he would be there for her all the way.

'Scusilo, aiuto. Chiami l'ambulanza. Questa donna ha bisogno dell'aiuto.' *Excuse me, help. Call the ambulance. This woman needs help.* Angelo shouted, looking to the front, watching the operator call the ambulance and talk to the driver, who instantly turned the boat around. They need to head northeast, to the other side of Lido. The vaporetto worker let Angelo know that there was an ambulance on the way, and that everything would be alright, the whole time staying a distance from the two, trying not to get in the way.

Angelo turned his attention to his stranger. She made quiet noises, nothing like a woman in labor. Jen tried to stop it; she kept her legs together like a child waiting for the bathroom, held her breath, prayed. Jen knew that it was not the time to resist and be embarrassed. She couldn't help it, it was her nature. She looked up at the ceiling of the bus, constantly taking deep breaths that she would hold as long as she could and concentrated intently on pushing all thoughts from her mind.

Standing above her, Angelo took in every detail that was this stranger. Her hair partially covered her face with sweat that dampened it. She looked relaxed as though she was meditating - calm and collected. This would have confused him, but her eyes betrayed the rest of her face and gave away her true feelings; fear, worry and hope. When he looked into her eyes, he knew that she didn't see him. She looked right past him as though she was looking into a different world. He looked down at her body and the swelling that would be her child. He looked past; she had her feet on the seat and her knees pointed to the ceiling. He couldn't help but notice that her sundress had slid down, which revealed the length of her white creamy thighs. So concentrated on her, he did not realize that he was repeating over and over again, 'it will be alright.' His hand was clutched tight to hers and his thumb caressed the backside of her hand.

'Ahhhh ...' A small painful sound came from her slightly opened mouth. And for a short moment in time, she looked into his eyes, and he looked into hers. Both enthralled in the deepness of what each person had to offer. He offered her comfort and strength and she offered him vulnerability and truth. This moment was something neither of them had ever felt, it would be remembered. It was intimate and desperate. For this short moment, he had become her lover, an angelic guardian, and her future.

Jen was the first to look away. She knew that this stranger was in, he could not leave her. Tears warped her vision. It was not the possibility of death that frightened her. The thought that her child would go through life without anyone, or not even have the chance to go through life frightened Jen. Maybe this was just Jen being selfish. She wanted to be with her child no matter what-she wanted to hold her creation.

Jen's free hand went to her belly. Her body screamed at her, just as her child would be any time now.

'Thank you.' Her small voice said in the direction of the stranger. She began to push, breathe and push.

Why wasn't her husband here? Angelo thought in an immediate anger. He knew if he ever saw that man, their meeting would not be a good one. Angelo broke from his thoughts as he realized he didn't even know this young girl's situation. For all he knew the father could be dead, or waiting back at the hotel she was staying at.

Angelo placed the back of his palm on her forehead. She felt too warm, but it could have also been the weather that made her so hot. Angelo started to feel nervous. He looked up and around him. Emergency vehicles were surrounding the boat. *Finally.* It had only been a short while, but to him it had seemed like an intimate eternity.

Two emergency attendants stepped onto the water bus. 'Qui.' Angelo shouted. Within minutes, she was bundled up safely in the ambulance, still in an eerie silence. No one questioned Angelo when he stepped into the ambulance and snuggled up to his stranger. She held out her hand for him to hold, and from her lips appeared a hint of a smile. The baby was born on the way to Ospedale de Mare in Lido. It was only for a few seconds but the young women stopped breathing. Angelo was unsure if it was the paramedic that gave back her breath or that he was breathing enough for both of them.

Her eyes opened. Gasping for life, the scene around her seemed to be a calm hectic, slow motion action. She looked up to the two men, one she recognized as her stranger, the other as the paramedic covered in blood. Where was her baby? She looked around and couldn't see or hear it. Something greater then herself forced her into unconsciousness.

An Ironic lullaby

Chapter Two

It is odd. It is odd that some people have the ability to love and give love so freely. To love someone almost instantly doesn't make much sense. To love someone before you truly know them, well I thought that was impossible. Not only for me, but also for the rest of the world. It is how the world worked. Maybe some people's ability to discover a person quickly results in an unquestioning easy love. Unsure of what it was did not mean it didn't exist. A stronger bond than any love is agape, unconditional. I feel this towards the little boy now… I wrap my arms around the little boy. He smiles. He is innocent, and I will spend the rest of my days to keep him as such. It is because of this little boy that I stay, it is because of him that I live the way I do. However, this is not my story, I feel, nevertheless, that it is left for me to tell.

Jen's eyelids felt heavy, but were ready to open. The beeping machine around her was almost as annoying as a silent ticking of a clock, yet unrecognizable. Her real panic, heightened with the rate of her heart as she felt the lack of her pregnancy. She never felt alone in Italy until now.

Around her darkness prevailed. She let her breath go into the unknown. What could she recall? A pair of eyes. A sturdy hand. A soft scent. She couldn't even think properly. No one was there. There was nothing left for her. Had she imagined the whole thing, this stranger? Someone she knew her whole life? Fuck, this was right out of a movie, but no, it was her real life, the situation she put herself into. The room started to show its shadows and give itself away. However, her only concern was for the life form that had sprouted from inside her.

Around her was an erie feeling. The lack of any other sound, aside from the beeping; the lack of a life form from inside; and the lack of a stable mind, developed a nightmare. The shadows started to dance… Sit up, get out of this bed, move to the light switch, reveal. The floors were cold against her bare feet, but it was refreshing, it was the only thing that felt real. As Jen walked a little further, she became aware of the cords that were hooked into her, but she did not care as she ripped them from her. Long beep. Oops! She hurried to the door and flicked on the light switch. The brightness washed her vision away.

Search, searching… so incoherent, panic, instinct… spotted… smile.

Jen swallowed hard as she was allowed her first look at her child. The child was laid out beside her, the whole time, in the darkness, an arms length away. He was beautiful- asleep and silent, his face relaxed and smooth. This is her child, so tiny, so innocent. His fingers were pulled away in little fists, which made Jen smile, and laugh. Wishing his hand was wrapped around her finger. 'You…' Jen whispered, the word hardly coming out. Gasps of air, of sighs kept coming out. She reached for his hand. 'Ragazzo,' the label read. She touched his skin, so soft. Jen's newly found mother instincts turned on as she felt an irresistible urge to hold him, to feel him and to love him. Tears welled up in her eyes; she had never experienced this unconditional feeling before. Her tears melted into laughter as she placed her other hand to his face.

Jen was interrupted by a burst of the hospital doors. Two young woman rushed around her, forcing Jen back into her bed.

'Stop this, I just want to be with my child.'

One nurse stayed with Jen as the other crossed to the other side of the room. She followed the nurse with her eyes, and stopped short of breath when she saw her stranger asleep in a chair. He had been there the whole time and she hadn't even noticed? The young nurse gently stirred him awake from his sleep.

'Che cosa e esso? E giusta?' What is it? Is she all right? He spoke soft and swift in a worried tone. Jen couldn't help notice his concern for her. Although she didn't completely understand what he said, she understood completely his tone of voice. Had anyone ever felt that way for her? It was a question she truly couldn't answer. Jen watched silently as a conversation went on between him and the nurse. What was going on? She wanted to know.

Suddenly the conversation was broken as Angelo looked over at his stranger and caught her eyes. Angelo instantly stood and was at her bedside in seconds. His hand raveled with hers and his lips to her forehead. 'Are you all right?'

'Yes.' Jen said surprisingly. Am I all right? Why did I say yes? It was because he was there. The warmth of this mans lips on her forehand, and his hand in hers. 'I… want to hold my baby.' She looked over at her child, who still slept, unknowingly. Her boy had not yet seen her face, and Jen wondered if he would even recognize her as his mother. Did he feel alone right now? Maybe he isn't waking up, because he isn't sure that there will be someone there to love him. Maybe he would never wake up. He needed to know, Jen's child needed to know that she was there, that she would always be there.

'I just woke up, I…I feel fine.' She lied. Her head hurt even more then it had when she first woke up, and her body felt weak and dizzy. She wasn't going to fight. 'Can I hold his hand?'

'I shall ask.' He turned once more to the nurses. This time the conversation had been successful. Jen knew this when she saw the nurses nod and leave the room.

'Thank you.' She whispered softly when her stranger came near. She fell asleep after a few moments of stroking the boys' hand lightly with the tips of her fingers.

Angelo smiled when he saw her drift into a heavy sleep. Her sweet lips curled upwards and her hand cradling her creation. Angelo only imagined that he knew what she felt towards her son, which made him wonder about his mother.

It had been seven days since he met her. He was with her even when she wasn't. It had been a long seven days. She had her baby about three minutes before they reached the hospital, at which point she had stopped breathing, was revived then passed out. Once they had reached the hospital, he had been separated from her. He sat in the waiting room, knowing nothing, but patient nonetheless. A few minutes past as though it were the last five minutes of his life. His brain had convinced him that there was no hope, that she would die. It touched him in an odd way that he cared so much. When he asked the question as to why he cared so much, it surprised him that he knew the answer: she needed him, and in some strange way, he needed her. After five minutes of patiently waiting, he went to the receptionist; 'I may not be her family yet, but I am her fiancée, I need to be with her.' That took care of it. The receptionist asked him to wait as she made a phone call. Jennifer is in room 221. The receptionist smiled, pleased with herself.

'Thank you.' Angelo said as he walked away. He smiled; it was only partially a lie. He did need to be with her. It was an unsaid promise that he needed to keep to her, Jennifer. Her name was Jennifer, she was no longer his stranger, she was now much more. Later that night, Jennifer was diagnosed with severe Eclampsia which, ever so often, threw her spontaneously into seizures. Angelo was asked to leave the room and was given an explanation from the doctor. There was nothing Angelo could do but hold her hand, somehow he knew that it must have helped. Her chances of death were greater than her chances of survival.

'Signor Piangotta,' the doctor spoke softly looking away, almost as though he was talking to someone else, 'I am to understand that Signora Jennifer has no insurance, and we have no records that she has the money to cover…'

'There is no need to worry, I will cover any expense.' The doctor nodded as Angelo walked away. This is never mentioned again.

For the next seven days, Angelo spends the majority of his time beside her bed holding her hand, never receiving any hint of her fate. Whenever he was not at the hospital, he spent his time thinking or talking of Jennifer. The first night when she was admitted to the hospital Angelo spent the night, he didn't make it home until the next afternoon. His family worried because he never called and they eagerly awaited any news on the will. Worried as his mother and four sisters were they forgave him as he relayed the whole event, leaving nothing out. When they found out, they all treated it as though they were responsible to help. It was demanded by his mother that they all visit her and the child the next day. This is where I first met her, on the verge of death, yet she was still the most beautiful person she had ever seen. Bellezza disonno, is what they say.

The second day Jen still stayed away from the world, aside from her spontaneous seizures, oblivious to her current situation and to anyone around her. Angelo came back everyday and started staying the night, his hand in hers. Something told him that she knew he was there watching over her, she needed to be touched. Then he couldn't go home at night, it was not even an option.

It was the sixth night, which Jen first slept through without having a seizure. And the seventh when she first woke up. He condition fragile but stable.

Jen woke up gently the next morning as though she simply had a good nights sleep. Her head no longer hurt like the night before. Her hand still holding her child, she sat up slowly so she could see her child more clearly. *You are mine, I am yours.* Nothing could have ever prepared Jen for the feeling she held within her body, a feeling she could only ever share with her boy, her blood, her life. In the distance, she could hear the music of a side café entertainment. A lute. A smile for her dream.

'What are you going to name him?' A voice she recognized more than any other drew her attention to the other corner of the room. It was the only voice she recognized, she couldn't recall any other, those she left at home. She slowly looked over at him and smiled.

'I am not so sure.' She looked back at the baby. 'I would like to hold him first.' This was the first time she really had an undisturbed, clear look around the room. It was small but comfortable. Light and soft. Jen's surprise came when she saw that there was no counter space left. The whole room was filled with toys and baby care items. She gasped across from her was a basket full of clothes and diapers.

Confusion spread across her face. *No one even knows that I am here, I don't even know where here is.* Her eyes were no longer clear as her salty tears fell. Behind her was a card labeled; 'It's a boy.' There must have been some sort of mistake. Not all this was for her, she had no one. Jerry would never have done something like this even if he had known, and her father probably forgot she even existed.

She picked up the card, inside it read, 'a beautiful boy for a beautiful mother.' signed 'your stranger.' Jen looked up to see him sitting close beside her. She hadn't even noticed that he had moved. Speechless. None of this made sense, no one in her life would do this for her, but her stranger? This was someone she had just met, someone that was with her for the most difficult part of her life. Someone she owed a great debt to- what could she say?

'Do you like?' He smiled nervously. His question almost made her laugh. Do I like it? She had ever received this most pure, honest gift. She did not deserve this. Her heart melted and sank at the same time. What is expected of me? What should I do? She looked at her stranger, still unable to speak. Instead of nodding, she started shaking her head.

'You do not like?' His voice and face filled with confusion.

'No, no, I love it...' She reached out to his hand. 'Its just that I never... I don't deserve this.'

Angelo could not believe what he was hearing. This woman had no one, the father to this child and her family was absent. *Was this a part of their culture?* Angelo remembered back to when his sisters had their children everyone was there, it was their unsaid mandatory attendance. Jennifer needed this more then anything, she needed something, some sort of support and this was his way of showing it.

'If you truly believe that you do not deserve this, then believe that your child does.' he looked over at the peaceful bundle.

'You are right, I'm sorry for being so selfish.' She hugged him. *Who does this women think that she is?* Angelo thought. By the way she was talking it sounded as though she thought very little of herself. *She must have been hurt.* And Angelo could only hug back.

'No, no, not true.' He knew there wasn't much he could do to talk her out of these odd thoughts. 'Besides this is not all from me, also from my mother and sisters. They have been here a bit.'

Jen did not think it odd that his family came to visit her. It comforted her to know that there were people, even if she didn't know them.

'I don't even know your name.' Pure shock.

'Angelo.' He responded. His name is Angelo; he is no longer a stranger.

'Mine is Jen.'

Angelo smiled; 'yes I know.'

'How long have I been here?' She had no concept of time, and yet it didn't really seem to matter.

'You have been here for eight days.'

Eight days. She had been out for over a week. She missed the first eight days of her child's life. This thought made her feel as though she was choking. When Jen was old enough to understand that her mother had past away during childbirth, she made a secret promise to herself. Her promise was her dedication to her child. It felt for a moment that promise she had made as a child was already broken. As soon as this thought came it left. She was alive, she had been beside him physically, and in some sort of way, she was also there for him spiritually. Although Jen never knew her mother personally, she was inspired by her. Jen was driven by a force, and when anyone would ask her what that force was, she replied; 'my mother.' The people she told knew her well enough to know that Jen never knew her mother.

Jen wanted to be that force with her child. She wanted a connection that only the two of them would understand. She needn't worry it was there just as the music that played out on the streets. The music louder now being quickly carried by the wind through the slightly opened window, there was a fulfillment in the moment. If it was a movie she lived in, it was a corny one.

Angelo sat, silently watching the transformation on Jen's face. He had not known exactly what was going through her thoughts, but he could see the emotion on her face. Jen wore her emotions without any concealment. A story always appeared for those who truly saw her. No masks.

This is when Angelo first discovered that words were not the only way to get to know a person. He felt he knew her and yet they had only shared a few phrases. He watched the way she slept, and when she was awake, he watched her watching her son and I watched him. All these little things added up. However, the largest thing that Angelo noticed about Jen was what she was capable of. It had been a year since his father had passed away. This death made Angelo rethink his life. He stopped painting, and he no longer saw beauty in simple things. He threw away what he had as a passion to women that truly meant nothing to him. He accepted a job that made him hate himself increasingly every day. The moment he laid eyes on this young women he saw true beauty, raw and genuine. *I wish it could have been me*. However, it was over the last eight days that sincerely tested him. He began to see beauty in the simple things. He heard the music and saw Venice as what it really was. Most importantly, he began to paint again. He tried to hide it, telling no one, but I couldn't help but watch. When he was away from the hospital by himself, he would paint something simple, a curtain blowing in the wind or a single artist playing a violin. When he was at the hospital he sketched small notepad sketches- Jens mouth or her hand, her closed eyes or her hair. True beauty.

Jen and Angelo both said nothing as they shared a moment. The moment was disturbed when a nurse burst through the door with a tray of food. She placed the food over Jen's lap and moved her bed upright so that she could eat. The nurse was someone that Jen did not recognize as one of the nurses she had seen the night before. This nurse had a kind look about her. She smiled as though she enjoyed her job, and had a gentle spirit. The nurse checked the baby and nodded in satisfaction. Before she left, she muttered something in Italian and stood silently expecting an answer.

'She wants to know if you have thought of a name for your son.' Angelo translated.

'Oh, yes.' Jen said proudly. She looked over at the nurse as though she was going to say something, and then paused looking back over at Angelo, 'I leave the decision up to you.'

'I… how about… Marcello.' Angelo replied almost immediately. 'The name of my father, who passed away a year ago to the day your child was born.'

'Marcello,' Jen looked at the nurse, who smiled and left. Jen smiled. One gift to another. Jen had never received a gift as wonderful as what Angelo offered her, it was likewise with Angelo.

'Thank you.' His voice came out softly. He was crying. Someone would have to look close at him to know that he was. A crack in his mask. It felt, in that moment, that he had given something back to his father, even if it was too late. For the last year, he felt numb, as though he could no longer feel. A year's work of emotion hit in a moment.

'It is the least that I can do.'

Jen and her child were allotted to leave on the ninth day. As she left the hospital, her thoughts morphed back to what made her go to Lido in the first place. The days in the hospital Jen had not worried about her future. She had not even once worried about money or getting home. As she felt the sun upon her face, worry hit her hard.

Upon leaving, Angelo brought his sisters and mother to help move all of Jen's gifts. Angelo carried the heavy basket and Jen had Marcello in her arms. Together the group took a private taxi boat from Lido to the San Marco area. Jens hotel was approachable through a canal access, which Jen never had the chance to use before. She felt as though she was someone important.

Angelo spoke to his family; Jen smiled, not knowing what was being said. It was hard for her to listen to a different language and not know what was going on. She felt as though she had a crutch. She looked away pretending that she wasn't listening.

The boat slowly glided to the docks of her hotel. Jens heart started to beat loudly; it washed out all conversation that was going on around her. Angelo got out of the boat first and then helped

Jen out. This moment made Jen feel as though she was a part of a different planet. Questions poured through her mind; *what am I going to do? Where will my baby and I go? How will we make it home?* And most urgent, *How will I pay for the hotel?* Her heart was sinking. Everything was drowning out, the sounds of the lute playing at a distant café.

Jen felt trapped when Angelo opened the door for her. It was her last chance she could run. Run. There was no place to go but through the door. When she stepped through a rush of familiarity washed over her. The receptionist was an older man, stout, with a well-tailored suit. She was reminded of her first day here. She was scared, as she felt now, a feeling that kept haunting her. She had come a long way, to make a full circle and come back.

If the receptionist recognized Jen, his demeanor showed no signs of it.

'Excuse me...' Jens voice was weak and small. She cleared her throat. 'I was staying here about nine days ago... for a few weeks in room 208...' She didn't know what to say next. 'I have not been here for nine days because...' Jen couldn't finish. She paused and the receptionist started speaking Italian to her. This confused Jen as he had spoken English perfectly well to her every time she needed to speak to him prior. He flared his arms around as though he was gesturing, which could have been because he was angry or trying to explain something. Either way Jen stared at him wide-eyed and overwhelmed. Her subconscious had her take a step back, and bump into Angelo. She knew he was still there. Did she have to ask him for help or was she too proud?

Angelo watched Jen try to communicate with the receptionist, who relayed that he was by no means responsible for anything. Angelo wanted to laugh, this man was trying to either take advantage of Jen, or really had no idea what he was doing. However, Angelo quickly glanced over at Jen who was staring back it him. Her eyes full of worry, her knuckles turned white and she clutched her hands around her child. Standing there so vulnerable, it reminded Angelo of a flute that stood alone in an orchestra during a solo. He wanted to take her away.

Angelo's voice resonated above that of the receptionist. Speaking loudly, quickly, and to the point. He said what Jen was trying to say in a matter of seconds. At the end of the conversation, Angelo passed the receptionist three Euros, and the receptionist passed over the few things that Jen had left in the hotel. As quickly as Angelo spoke, he led her away from the pit stop of her life.

Jen was stagnant, staring, and unsure of her own mind. Standing on the other side of the world, and being taken care of better than she ever had before. Marcello brought her back to reality, she was following Angelo's lead with his hand placed on the small of her back. He sat her down on a bench, which sat naked in front of the sky. Unsure of what he was doing, Jen faced Angelo who sat down beside her. A moment went by that only a hum of life around them was heard. Angelo looked uneasy, as he moved in closer beside her. Jen couldn't help but notice his knee brushing up against hers.

'I guess that this is good-bye.' Jen tried to look at him, but ended up facing away, the breeze forced her hair to blow across her face. It was an odd feeling, getting to know someone, and then letting that person go. All in travel. All in life. A hand cupped around her cheekbone gently caressing her face. She turned to look back at this man with the soft touch. Her eyes started to tear up, yet she made no notice of it.

'Do you want it to be?' He spoke slowly, and rough rather than soft. His voice was alluring. Jen shifted her eyes to look past him, it was as though he was drawing her into another world. He spoke before she could reply. 'What I am saying is, you are more than welcome to stay with my family and I.' He finally said what he wanted to for sometime. However, he was unsure of her situation and didn't want to push it upon her. It made him nervous, the thought of her saying no. Her situation no longer mattered as she said good-bye - if he didn't ask now, he would never be able to.

'Can I do that?' Jen asked more to herself than anything. She needed this, but her thoughts were getting in the way. Pride, self-acceptance, and nerves.

'Yes you can.'

'Your family would be okay with me staying?' She couldn't actually believe that she was even thinking about it as an option.

'Yes, my mother even suggested it.' He paused smiling. 'They would help you with the baby, and keep you in good company.'

'Would you be okay with me staying?' Jen already knew the answers to the questions she asked but needed to buy time to think about the offer.

'I don't understand the question. I would not offer if I do not mean it.'

'I'm sorry I didn't mean...'

'No that's all right.' Angelo interrupted, 'there is no need for an apology. The house is of fair size, and we have an extra room for you. You can stay as long as you need. I would love having you there.' He spoke with such sincerity it made Jen blush. 'I have feeling you say yes.' He laughed.

'I don't know... know what to say.' Pause. 'This is...' She couldn't cry, she already looked weak as it was, she cleared her throat before she spoke again. 'This offer is amazing.' Deep breath. *Can I say yes?*

'Say yes.' Angelo almost read her mind.

A small smile spread across her face. She had made up her mind, 'all right. The answer is; yes.' She eased, she felt as though she could relax for the first time since leaving the hospital. 'I don't know how to show my appreciation, all I have to offer back is my thanks.'

'Then I accept.' Relief swept through Angelo, he didn't have to say good-bye, at least not yet. What if she would have said no? The thought that she might have came when she started asking questions. He would miss her if she would have declined, and beyond that, he would miss himself.

'Then let us not delay.' Angelo helped Jen up. 'My family is waiting.' Together they walked back to the boat. Jens legs felt weak, Angelo was there for her support. Whatever nerves went through her body disappeared as she looked at the decreasing distance of his family and noticed all of them cheering. Jen had to laugh, never in a million years. She was going to live in a real home in Venice. She looked down at her sleeping child. He was safe, her little Marcello was safe.

When she got into the boat with his family, all took turns to welcome her. Cheers. Overwhelmed as Jen was, she disguised her low self-esteem inside and stood tall.

Angelo was overwhelmed as well. He wanted to ask her situation for curiosity sake, but knew that she would tell him in due time.

The boat slowly pulled away from the dock. Jen looked back, 'regret nothing' she silently whispered to herself, 'regret nothing.' A deep breath, and no more looking back. She was letting go of the life she knew before. The boat went slowly through the Canals, through the maze, until it opened into the Grand Canal. As they passed the Rialto, Jen looked at the little café she had sat at, and noticed a woman sitting where she had just day's prior. This woman sat alone, and for a brief moment, Jen wondered if she looked like her. However, she was a Venetian, and Jen was not. The boat left the Grand Canal that flowed into the Giudecca Canal. Angelo lived on the south side of Isola della Giudecca. The wind hit instantly upon Jens face as when they turned west to go around the island to shortcut through Rio S. Biagio. Through the Canal, the boat passed Ex Monastero della Maddalena, and went east. Angelo and his family had spent their lives in this area. It was a silent trip for Jen, any questions that went through her mind she discarded, she would obtain all her answers in due time.

Jen's nerves slowly morphed into a hidden excitement. She looks around the buildings that surrounded her. Any one of these places could be his, but which? As the boat kept going, her excitement grew. What seemed like forever to Jen was dismissed as the boat turned into a beautifully gated archway leading into a water like piazzetta. The house vaulted around the open area, which made it their only private area. The walls covered in vines of green leaves and purple flowers at the peak of the season. What was left of the uncovered walls, showed the buildings true age, and history. This appealed to Jen, as it looked the way it should in its natural growth. Each room looked as though it faced into the piazzetta. It was a tall slim house, three stories high. *Did he own all of this? This is not real, is it? Am I dreaming?*

A young man stood at the edge of the stoned pathway to help everyone out of the boat. Jen hadn't heard of him, Angelo hadn't told her there was anyone else. Is he the butler? He seemed too young, however as though he should still be in school. Jen followed the family into the house, which looked like a dream. The air even seemed misty, and candles kept the entrance hallway dimly lit. A partitioned wall kept her from seeing the heart of the home. Two steps to the right, and floods of light poured in through the huge arch openings. Wooden shutters and hand made glass windows were the only protection from the outside world, which were left wide open. Everything in the room was touched by a soft array of light, which made everything feel warm. When Jen stepped forward more into the room, the sunshine poured onto her. It had its own sensation. The further she walked in, the more unlikely she thought that this place could be reality. Each piece in the room was its own masterpiece, all hand created and properly cared for. Small paintings enchanted the room with life and magic. Jen had never seen work quite like it before and wondered if the pieces were originals or not.

Jen found she was looking past the inside of the house to the back area of the home, large windows opened to catch a clear view of the Gulf of Venice. She was looking out onto the Mediterranean Sea. A place of history, a place where dreams must have come true. She could stand there for an eternity, a place where she could forget everything she needed to. Creations and visions of her dreams came to her. She could feel Angelo watching her, he watched her eyes. Watching her eyes was better than looking at the view. Because through her eyes was the view through the way she saw it, including the emotion she felt about it.

'This is all you need to know about life.' He whispered. What Jen saw and felt at that moment she could never forget - this was satisfaction in the greatest sense.

Angelo shared the moment, his feelings the same but for a different reason. His view was that of a beautiful woman of mystery, of love, of wonders. Cradled in her arms a masterpiece, a child, sound asleep, peaceful. Through an artist's eyes, through the eyes of the heart.

One Knock, Three Lives

Chapter Three

The first time I met her was at the hospital; however, the first time she met me was her first day at the home. I watched her looking out over the Gulf of Venice. I watched Angelo watch her. Angelo saw me and asked me to come over.

'Jennifer, this is Kate. She works here, and will help you with anything that you need.'

'Boungorno... ah... ' She was trying to find the words.

'That is alright I don't speak Italian very well, I speak English.' I stepped in right away.

' You are Australian.' Jen smiled. I could tell that she instantly felt comfortable around me. 'And then this is Marcello.'

I liked her, and I could tell that she liked me. We could confide in each other, we could be there for each other. I just knew. I knew that she could be there for me, but maybe I didn't know myself enough to realize that I wouldn't be able to be there for her. I was too lost in myself...

The first few days at the house were the hardest. Four days had past, and not only did Jen have to acquaint herself with everyone, but she also had to find where everything was, and learn how to take care of a child. She had heard horror stories about doing something wrong with the baby, and was determined to prevent any of them at all costs. Jen had been gifted with a room on the third story that had balconies on both sides - one that opened into the piazzetta and the other that looked out over the gulf. She liked standing on both balconies; they both gave her different feelings. One gave her the feeling of being out and open to the world, a world filled with endless possibilities. The other balcony she felt comfortable and safe, she felt protected as though nothing could ever disturb her. There she created her own little world.

Jen had hardly seen Angelo in those four days. Yet he was always went out of his way to ask her if she was doing well, but then would leave swiftly, without explanation.

The last time she had seen him, he had knocked on her door early that morning. She thought it would be Kate so she didn't cover her nightgown with a housecoat before she answered the door. She quickly regretted that when she saw who was at the door and her face flushed red. She snatched up her housecoat and slipped into it.

'How are you doing?' He laughed. She was modest. She gestured for him to step into the room, and he did. 'I trust that you enjoy it here.'

Jen looked around her room; it was full of everything the family had sent to her during her stay in the hospital. 'Everything is perfect.'

Before she could ask him anything, he walked away saying, 'have a nice day.'

Jen was starting to wonder about Angelo's thoughts. Is he taking his feelings back? Does he wish he never offered me a place in his home? Maybe his staying away from her and their brief conversations was his way of saying 'good-bye.' She couldn't tell and her thoughts became agony. She wished she could shrug it away, but how?

Over the first few days everyone except Angelo's mother, Caprice was shy of her. She helped her out the best she could, even though she could hardly speak English. She took care of the baby when Jen needed to use the rest room or shower. And in return, Jen kept Caprice company in the kitchen, and helped her prepare the food each evening while Marcello slept. Caprice made Jen feel at home, as she told stories of her life in Venice.

'Angelo's father was an amazing man,' Caprice gestured all around her, 'he gave me everything, he gave me the world.' Angelo's father, Marcello, had met Caprice while on a business trip from Rome. He sat around a table with three other men and couldn't keep his eyes off his server. Caprice even held traces of her youth,- classy, tall and stunning. Marcello moved his wealthy business to Venice to take a chance on this woman he knew nothing of. They fell in love, even though Caprice had nothing. Marcello was willing to risk everything for her, he stopped talking to his father who disapproved, and married the most beautiful person he had ever seen. Within the first five years of their marriage, they were blessed with five children. Angelo, Eleanora, Gemma, Serena, and Aria.

On the thirty-eighth year of knowing each other, Marcello passed away. This drew Angelo to come back and take care of Caprice and his four sisters. It made Jen wonder where Angelo was before and whether or not he wanted to be here anymore.

One story about Marcello and Angelo stuck out the most. 'Angelo's father he came to me one night with Angelo in his arms. Late in evening, tears pouring down his face.' Caprice paused trying to find the wording for English. 'He says to me, Angelo spoke,' I was shocked, 'he did?' I says back, 'yes, he said 'beautiful.' Sure enough Angelo had made an attempt at saying 'beautiful.''

This story made Jen wonder more about Angelo. She didn't even know what he liked, what made him happy, what made him hurt. Over the last few days, Jen learnt more about his father than about him. Yet, no one knew her better then Angelo, he knew what he needed to know just through the picture she painted in her eyes. Although they did not know each other's history, they connected at a deeper level.

On the fourth night, Caprice told Jen the relationship between Angelo and his father. It must have been the same between Angelo's father, Marcello, and his father. Marcello had never told Angelo how proud he was of him, and now he would never get that chance. Jen spoke little, she didn't want to ask questions, but it seemed the more she knew the more questions she had.

Meals were Jen's favorite part of the day. Everyone would be sitting around the table as they ate, talking, enjoying, congratulating. Jen never had this before; she never had a family who was at home. Angelo's sisters spoke little English, so many Italian conversations would keep circling around the table. Jen started understanding certain words, and when she was left alone she would take the time to look up words that she didn't know, until she could remember them.

The third week, everyone was fully captivated in their meal, however Jen was captivated with the paintings on the wall. She studied them deeply. Who is this artist? She wondered. Whoever it was had the capability of capturing the moment.

'Who is the artist to these paintings?' She had longed to ask since she arrived. There were no names on them, as if they were left unclaimed. Everyone became silent and still, only Angelo was aware enough to answer her.

'Why?' He stopped. 'Do you not know?' He leaned with his elbow on the table, with a small smirk on his face. 'What do these paintings do for you?'

'Well…' talk about being put on the spot. 'To be completely honest,' she paused, 'I believe, well, I feel the artist is confused, or wants to portray that to the person viewing the piece. Confused in a way of loneliness. Confused in a way of hope. This particular painting, the subject or the underlining artist, has just lost something. Something that had the ability to cast off one shot of a thought. This shot then becomes trapped into what we see in front of us. The detail painted on the hand shows the ability of one person's capability. The shades of greens and browns in the background not only promote a life style of health and beauty, but a distant comfort that is not yet in grasp because it is not clear but blurry. The lines on the hand show paths that the subject, or the artist, has the ability to take, and hasn't yet chosen. One path looks clear and long while the other has many turns and bends. Moreover, the viewer, knows before the artist does which path must be chosen. Whoever that person is must go down the unknown, because he can't take the easy way out.' Jen stopped, and took a deep breath of satisfaction. 'It is beautiful, really.'

The table was silent for what seemed to be a century, still and silent. Angelo sat in shock, how is it she is able to tell more about my painting than I can. A moment went by and his sisters continued to eat. His mother sat still and smiled, she had a knowing look in her eye. Both Jen and Angelo could see, but couldn't tell what it was.

'I'm sorry, am I wrong?' Jen asked.

'No, no, its just how do you know about this painting, it is as though you have seen it before.' Angelo spoke slowly.

' I have.' Jen replied, and began to eat again. She paused long enough for Angelo to contort to an ultimate confusion. 'I have come across it many times.'

'You have?' Caprice spoke on behalf of Angelo.

'Yes, well not physically but within myself.' She smiled sadly. 'I imagine if I could paint I would paint that. I look at this painting and it looks back at me.'

Angelo's face turned from confusion to being content, he understood. 'Why is it, you think, that what you said is what the painting actually means?' He continued to challenge her.

'Well I only say what I feel, it could be not on par with what the artist wants me to feel, but it is good enough for me.' She smiled at the evoked emotions that Angelo seemed to be going through.

'Good enough for me too.' Angelo replied slow and strong.

'So you never answered my question, who is the artist?'

Before Angelo answered, he smiled and looked over at his mother, she smiled back. 'I am.'

Jen almost dropped her utensils. She had just analyzed a painting to the artist, her face flushed instantly. She looked over at her child in a small crib placed close enough to reach her hand in. *Why can't Marcello sleep like this during the night?* Jen thought.

'I apologize.'

'For what?' He could hardly understand her sometimes.

' For analyzing your painting for you.'

'But I asked you to. Do not worry about such things.'

'Do not treat yourself so badly.' Caprice cut it. 'You are wondrous in you words.'

This also made Jen blush, she smiled shyly and said, 'thank you.' At which point one of Angelo's sisters, Eleanora, the eldest daughter, started to speak over everyone else in Italian almost shouting. Then simultaneously Gemma, Serena, and Aria started shouting in the same manner, one over the other.

Jen looked around, confused, and out of sorts. All the commotion woke up Marcello with a start. He started softly crying and slowly reached his maximum. Rather than being annoyed with him, she used his crying as an excuse to leave.

'Excusi, per favore.' Only Caprice and Angelo noticed her leave. Jen looked back around the room one more time, picked up her child and quickly left.

Angelo knocked softly at first then harder. He heard over his knocking a silent, 'come in,' so he followed the door into the room, and closed it behind him before he looked around to see where Jen was. His breath almost stopped and he swallowed hard at the sight of this woman. She had her back towards him, her shirt was partially off as she had the baby nestled up to her breast. Angelo saw the curve of her back uncovered and all he wanted to do was feel the softness that was her skin.

'Sorry, I…' He had no words, he wasn't sorry in the least. He wanted to respect her and leave, but he couldn't.

'No that's all right, just as long as you stay there.' She laughed. 'It's funny after having a child you don't care so much about modesty, you care more about the well being of your child.' She took her child back to the crib and pulled up her shirt, before turning to Angelo.

There was somewhat of an awkward silence. One of the silences where both wanted to induce in conversation, rather than discussing the subject that needed to be addressed.

'Look, I apologize for the behavior of my sisters… I cannot apologize for them as they do not feel they did anything wrong, however I apologize for their behavior.' He emphasized the 'I.' 'And I…'

'No, that's all right.' Jen said stepping forward. 'There is no need to apologize.' Jen knew what was happening. In the three weeks that she had been there, his sisters never once went out of their way to get to know her. The youngest, Aria, occasionally smiled at her in the hallways but the other three did not. Jen, on the other hand, spent many times trying to converse in Italian. Perhaps she had said something to offend one of them. They made her feel unwelcome, perhaps she was. Angelo had abandoned her daily. It was only Caprice that made her feel welcome.

'No it is not, please accept my apologizes.'

'All right, I accept.' That was the end of that conversation, he apologized, and she accepted.

The two stood still looking at each other. 'You feel happy here?' Angelo asked ,slightly nervous for her answer.

'Yes, oh there is no need to worry on my behalf.'

Angelo nodded as he stepped further into the room towards the cradle to where Marcello was, looking silently up at the ceiling. Angelo looked back at him and smiled. 'All right then have a good night.' He looked at Jen once more before he left the room.

Jen was left there, confused and worried. Something seemed different with him. Although she told him she was all right, all she really wanted to tell him was that she missed him. She missed him more than anything. They never talked any more, they only saw each other during meals that the family shared together, and when he was there, his mind was somewhere else. She missed what she knew of him.

She felt torn as to what to do. Apart of her wanted to run after him and tell him what she thought. However, the other part of her couldn't move. He had let her stay here and she didn't want to feel more selfish than she already was. Jen paused only for a moment. What she wanted got the best of her, no going back. She swung the door open, he needed to know this. As she opened the door, she noticed that Angelo still stood in the hallway facing her door, towards her.

'What are you still doing in the hall?' She asked him after a silent moment.

'Just looking at the door.' He said so naturally, as though nothing odd was happening. 'What are you doing in such a hurry?'

'I… just needed to get some fresh air in the room.' She almost fooled herself and was ready to shut the door on him, forgetting the actual reason for opening the door.

'Are you all right?' He stepped closer to her.

She smiled; 'well actually…' she pulled him into her room, and sat him down on her bed. 'I was planning to ask you that.' She closed the door behind her and leaned against it. 'Are YOU all right?'

'Why do you ask?' He asked slowly.

'Because, you seem much more distant since I moved in than at the hospital, and let it take the best from you. Its just that…'

He interrupted her with a violent lift of her to the bed and silenced her with a heavy kiss upon her mouth. This is not what she had expected. It may have been what she wanted, but this was beyond reality. She wanted to enjoy it, but at the same time, her conscience made her push him away.

'I apologize, I thought that this is what you want.' Angelo was bold with his words.

'It is.' She answered without hesitation, 'but I want you to address how you feel about me staying here. You don't seem to want me here.' Her honest, upright statement blew her away. She usually danced around these conversations.

He looked away, and Jen could not tell if he was upset or not. There was a long silence. 'I don't.'

That is why I was scared to ask. Jen reassured herself, - *it will be all right.* She didn't know whether to laugh or cry. She didn't know what to do. He simply didn't want her there; it was as simple as that. Nothing more. She sighed, and slightly shook her head. So, this is what reality was. Now she understood.

Angelo leaned forward. 'You must know...'

'Yeah, that's why I asked.' Jen interrupted.

'No,' Angelo laughed. 'You must know where I want you.' He stood. 'Come with me, Kate will watch over your child for you.'

Jen stood. What is happening? 'I need to take you somewhere.'

'Ah, okay.' Jen could hardly speak. 'Should I change?'

'Never.'

They both left the house. Walking swiftly. Through endless allies. What was happening? One moment he doesn't want me, the next I am following him into nowhere. Jen struggled to keep up. He held onto her hand. Wherever they went she followed, she would follow him anywhere. Her eyes began to water; her emotions were ready to explode. The swift walk must have gone on forever. Angelo seemed persistent, however, so the pace never changed. He led her away.

Finally he stopped. 'This is it.' They seemed to be in a shabby area. Full of ware houses that looked abandoned. Full of small paths and no lights.

'What do you mean?'

'This is it, come.' Angelo found a door to the warehouse they stopped at. He unlocked it and led her through the door. 'This is where I want you.' He says as he turns on the lights.

First Jen had to shield her eyes, but when her eyes adjusted, she almost fell over.

'Whose is this?' She asked only half listening, stepping in further.

'This is mine.' Proud and stern.

Jen took a moment to explore. She walked into the middle of the large room. His art studio filled with canvases and materials and finished artwork. Rows after rows of work. His work.

'Angelo, this is unbelievable.' Moments went by where she just stood looking around her. Angelo finally approached her from behind, silently and whispered in her ear. 'Would you like to see upstairs?'

Jen jumped but only for a moment, 'si.' He took her up to an open loft, looking over the art studio. The upstairs was filled with covered furniture, a partly renovated area.

'What is this for?' Jen asked.

'I hoped that it would be for us. I don't want you there, I want you here. With me.' He held her hand.

What an emotional roller coaster. 'What are you saying?' Jen understood, but she wanted to hear it from him directly.

'I am saying I want you to live in with me, I want you to stay with me.' He let go of her hand and ran to an area that looked like covered windows, and ripped down the white sheets, the view looked back to Venice. Venice at night is beautiful. The lights and the water, and the romance. The windows covered the wall.

'I can't believe this.'

'Believe it. Say something else.'

'Beautiful.'

'Tell me... I need to know... I want you to live with me, I want you to be with me, I want you to love me...' he paused, 'I want you to love me as much as I love you.' Jen couldn't say anything. 'Please say something.'

'I...' She was crying. 'I don't understand.'

Angelo grabbed both of her arms. 'Understand!' He smiled. 'Understand that I am in love with you.'

'But Angelo, you seemed so distant these last weeks, I thought that you were starting to regret letting me stay with you.'

'You must know... what may seem me being distant to you is only my way of trying not to fall in love with you.'

'Did it work?' Jen cut him off.

'No... every time I see you I want nothing more than to pick you up into my arms and comfort you and your pain. I...' he paused. 'I don't know who the father of your child is, but I know that he is not worth it, not worth what you are. In a few months, this place will be ours.'

Jen's heart was pounding uncontrollably. He was it, and this was it. Whatever uncontrollable circumstances got her to this point in her life was worth it, and meant to be. She was finally able to admit her love for him to her, and admit it to him.

'Please say something. When I found out that you might die in the hospital, I almost, I didn't know what to do. I knew that I couldn't live without you.'

'I love you...' she stopped, 'can I say that?'

He laughed and picked her up, 'of course you can.' She loved to hear him laugh. A really corny movie.

As Angelo gave her a tour of the upstairs, she couldn't believe that this was it. He even renovated a room for Marcello. He really meant it. This moment changed them both. Angelo would stop putting work before him; he would concentrate on art and look after his family. And Jen would stay, and live the life she always should have, to feel. After three months of knowing each other, Angelo and Jen would possess a romantic moment together. She would experience her first true love making moment. Both would be entangled in the motions and emotions they were gifted to share with each other. A moment that would never be forgotten, a moment that would change the rest of her life. It was only the beginning of her movie.

Legs Like Jelly

Chapter Four

Where did I belong? Everything always happened to the people around me. It seemed like I lived for them. I lived for her, for Marcello, for Angelo. It was the thought that I lived off of, during that time in my life. Not realizing I actually did have a life, for I too was away from home.

'Kate,' Jen turned her head towards me. Always so graceful. She was inspecting fruit from a little stand in the market right off the Rialto. And I felt like her follower.

'Yeah?' I diverted my attention from the distant sound of a boat. I loved watching the Vaporettos go by, full of people to watch. No matter what time of the year always packed with tourists.

'Can you hold Marcello for me?'

'Yeah, sure.' Jen passed her child to me. I held him before but this is the first moment I recall him touching me back. It felt as though Jen was more than passing him to me. I felt obsessed with his presence he felt like he was mine. This day Marcello was in an odd mood. I didn't even think that a child, at his age, could laugh, but he seemed to be laughing at everything. I smile back at him, and he reaches his little hand out towards me. I bring him closer and his hand touches my cheek, I smile. Never wanting to let go... not realizing I wouldn't be able to.

'He likes you.' Jen laughed. 'Don't you little one.' We continue walking through the busy market. People turn to look at her.

'I like him too.'

'It's nice to have you here.' Jen continued. 'I felt so unsure when I first came.'

'What do you mean?' I was confused. 'Why did you feel unsure?'

'I don't really know. It is nice to have someone to talk to.' This confused me even more - we hadn't conversed too much. I know now that she was asking me rather then telling me. She needed someone to talk to, and

she was asking me if it would be all right. She took Marcello back, who laughed. For some reason I felt stripped of what was mine, knowing that it wasn't in the least bit.

'Yes, it is nice to have someone to talk to.' We continued walking down the market. The day went by slowly in a graceful pace. It was wonderful knowing that such a beautiful women was so real... but she still felt like a dream.

'Do you love him?' I spoke before I thought.

'Yes, no, who?'

An awkward pause.

'The man who this child belongs.' I lied.

'Oh... no, I mean I thought I did, but... I think that I was lying to myself.' She stopped. I realized this must have been a touchy subject for her. But she continued. 'I haven't told him.'

'I'm sorry... '

'I never told him.'

'You never told him that you thought you loved him.'

'No sorry.' She shook her head, and came back to focus only on me and the child. 'I never told him about our child.'

'Don't you think that he has the right to know?'

Jen paused. 'Yes. I left him because I... ' Long pause. 'I didn't want to bother him with... I didn't want him to feel he had to do anything.'

'He should be happy... ' I didn't understand.

'Not with the situation. We broke up.' She paused and I could tell she was thinking strongly about what to say next. 'We were young, I mean we still are young. Something like this... ' She looked down at Marcello in her arms, '... makes you grow up pretty fast. But here I am... ' I could hear a giggle through her throat.

'If you don't mind me asking how old are you?' I should have stopped, I was being inappropriate. Why was I so curious? I would never really know.

'Eighteen.'

I stopped. Only eighteen. I didn't know what to feel. I tried to hide everything inside. Only eighteen. I remember eighteen, I didn't remember it being anything like that.

'I left, Kate. I left and I haven't turned back.' Her mind traveled to another life, one that was a mystery to me. Possibly a mystery to her as well. 'Let's go, shall we?' We had wondered around a lot that day, and I was tired. I can only imagine how Jen felt. We both shopped.

'Where are you going after you leave here?' Was the last thing I asked her on the taxi back to Guidecca.

'Angelo has asked that I stay with him when he moves to his paint studio. After that, life has no intentions on telling me until it happens.'

A streak of jealousy ran through me. There was no reason for it, except my feelings I shared for Angelo. I looked at her, and wanted to be her. I wanted to be her. I would take all her struggles from her, if only I could be her. I was happy for her, but sad for myself. How could I let this happen? I tortured myself.

'A new day brings a new moment.' I watched her step off the boat into the piazzetta and walk away. I looked over to my friend, Orazio, the butler. He smiled back. None of us noticed as Jen collapsed into a seizure, the child safe at her side. Cradling and crying in her shaking arms.

Jen woke up to her child crying. It was not a harsh cry, but a soft and gentle sob. She smiled, Marcello brought her back to the reality of the day ahead. As soon as reality hit her the dream-like quality of the night before was put aside. She removed the covers and instantly felt the warmth of the sun against her bare skin. Alone in her room, she didn't worry about covering her completely exposed body. She stood, feeling the tile against the bottom of her feet. The windows cracked open and the curtains blew into the room, the chill fell upon her body and rushed all the way through. A new sensation she never thought she could appreciate.

As she held the baby in her arms, she smiled and looked out into the Gulf. A mist filled the air, adding an extra moisture to her skin. It was a busy morning on the gulf, filled with life, men working and boats cruising by. This was the life, Jen thought watching. This is the life that anyone would ask for. She never stopped to think that for the men on the boats, this was the way they survived, not living their days in a dream like her.

'Don't cry little one, you are here, safe with your mom.' Jen kissed his forehead. 'We are in this together, you and I.'

She cradled him until he stopped crying.

Waking up to the crying didn't faze Jen - she was in a great mood. Marcello, a little life, a whole life she had cradled in her arms. The night before was also in her mind, she never knew. With Marcello in her arms she started softly singing, which started her to dance. Marcello started giggling.

She held Marcello out into the air and began to spin in circles. Jen nearly lost her step. A figure loomed at the opposite corner of the room at the other balcony, watching her with an intense focus. She immediately recognized this figure as Angelo, the tall broad shoulder man she was beginning to find comfort in. She quickly freed one arm and covered herself with a sheet.

There was a look of horror on Jen's face, which caught Angelo off guard. 'I am sorry.'

'I thought that you had left.' Her face flushed.

'Why don't you uncover yourself?' He stepped forward, smiling at her shyness.

'I… can't.'

'But I felt every inch of you last night.' He smiled. Another step.

'But it was dark.' Softly, nervously. She could not recall the time between Angelo's second step and his appearance on the same side of the room as her.

'But you are beautiful.'

'You don't have to… I under…'

'Why can't you believe that you are beautiful?' His voice rough and raw.

'What is beauty to you?' She challenged. A sudden change to her voice.

Angelo's eyes flared. His passion filled his aura. And he simply answered, 'you.'

'I'm not sure I believe you.'

This woman is impossible. 'Why do you challenge me?'

'Because to you…' she paused. 'Everything must be beautiful. I must be the same. It was your first word and it, I dare say, will be your last in years to come.' She stepped back.

'It is true that I find beauty in many things, it is true that it was my first word, but it is also true that you are my most true version of beauty.'

She looked down, hiding what she felt. He placed his hand on her cheek, caressing with his thumb. 'Have you ever felt this before?' He slowly slid his hand from her cheek down her neck across her shoulder and down her back. 'My hands know your beauty. Do you see me looking at you?'

'Yes.'

'Can't you see their reflection of you?'

'I am sorry, it is hard…' Jen stepped back.

'What did he do to you?' Angelo even surprised himself. He tried asking where the father was many times, but he didn't want to feel as though he was pushing her away.

Jen hesitated, 'nothing.' No more.

Angelo went back to the other side of the room. This was the first time that Jen noticed all of his things. Against the chair was a case full of paints, and a blank canvas resting in his easel.

'Can I paint you?' He asked, but he was already setting up his paints.

'Am I good enough?' Jen asked nervously.

'You are perfect.'

Jen blushed again, 'All right, how?'

Angelo approached her again, this time, placing Marcello back in the cradle. He held her wrist as he guided her to the bed, he had her recline on the bed, partially covered by the sheet and the rest of her skin exposed to the warm air.

What am I getting myself into? Tell him no, you can't do this. She was nervous, however Angelo did all he could to make her feel comfortable. How often does he do this? How many women? Jen couldn't help but think. She tortured herself with these thoughts constantly.

They spent the whole day in the room. The only time he was disturbed was when he asked Orazio to bring up fruit and cheese. Angelo painted her, occasionally stopping to check on Marcello and kiss Jen, before he would get back to the canvas.

When he finished his painting he made love to her.

'Can I see it?' Jen asked nervously. He was to show her his masterpiece. She is the masterpiece. Angelo had captivated his feelings and her true beauty in painting. He was nervous, just as she was. For a long time she looked at the painting and was quiet. Angelo almost couldn't take it. He watched her as she watched the painting. Her eyes filled with tears, almost unnoticeably.

'I see me through your eyes.' She paused and smiled. 'I see me through your eyes; I see how beautiful I am.' Angelo succeeded.

'You will make a year of pay when you sell this painting.' She laughed hugging him. There was a confidence in her voice, in her eyes, something she had lacked before.

'I do not intend on selling it.' Angelo smiled. 'It is mine to keep.'

'I give you permission to do what you need to do.' Free. She felt as though this painting made her free. She held no restrictions within herself. Free with her body, and mind.

Jen woke up the next morning much in the same matter. Still tingling from the touch of Angelo the night before, she made her way over to Marcello. He needed to be fed, once again his little vocal chords pressed hard and a drilling cry could be heard. Jen picked him up, and he immediately found where he needed to go to feed. 'Hush little baby, don't say a word, mama's going to buy you a mockingbird ...' Jen sang. No matter what happened, they had each other.

She sensed once again that there was someone in the room, she turned to look at the chair where Angelo loomed the morning before, however it was vacant. She laughed to herself and only thought that she was getting paranoid. She turned back to the cradle and that is when she noticed her. Caprice's Eldest daughter, Eleanora, leaning against the door. Quickly Jen covered herself with a sheet. What was she doing? Jen felt a feeling of nervousness wash over her. Eleanora laughed as she stepped forward.

'I trust you slept well.' She laughed again.

This made Jen feel uneasy, yet Jen reacted as though nothing was out of the normal, 'Yes, thank you.'

'Look, wasting time.' Eleanor couldn't even speak English well enough, but she was able to get by. Jen wanted to laugh, over the last three months she had learnt enough Italian to understand the conversations at the table, and was able to speak fluently. 'You should find a job quick, get money, leave.'

Jen stood there confused. She had felt that Eleanora never liked her. She was cold from the beginning. Yet, Jen mistakenly thought that they had made an unsaid agreement.

'Sorry, I am not quite sure that I understand you.' Jen stepped back with her wave of emotion.

'You are no longer welcome here, we ask you leave as soon as possible.'

Jen sat down on the edge of the bed, looking at little Marcello. What is happening?

'We hear cries of a whore at night.' Eleanora stepped forward trying to grab between Jens legs. Jen stood.

'That is not true.' Her voice apparently louder and defensive. Her heart leaping out of her chest.

'Leave.' Eleanora left, with what seemed like no emotion on her face, slamming the door behind her.

Jen sat, that's all she could do. Exhausted and worn from the conversation she had just suffered. The feeling odd. It was this moment where Jen went from her ultimate high point in her life to her ultimate low point, all in a matter of seconds. She looked down at little Marcello, and wanted to cry. The tears never came, yet a cold feeling shivered through her. Jen thought back to the moments in which she had been with the sisters. Eleanora and Gemma, the two older sisters, made it blatantly obvious that Jen was not welcome. However there was Caprice, Kate and Angelo to counterpart it. She was unsure of the two younger daughters, Serena and Aria.

'Don't worry little one, everything will be alright.' She wasn't sure who she was actually talking to, her child or herself.

An hour passed by where she sat there, unsure of what to do, holding Marcello. She had acted on an irrational idea, and now she was left here, to once again think irrationally.

Before Jen did anything else, she looked out to the Gulf - it was a beautiful day. Today reminded her of that day she went to Lido and fell asleep on the beach. She was back to the beginning. She slowly left her room, with caution, not wanting to run into Eleanora, or anyone. She wanted to get out of the house. As she gently closed the door behind her she saw Aria at the end of the hall. Aria smiled and nodded her head gently. Jen turned her head, unsure of what was going through Aria's thoughts, but not wanting to challenge them.

She almost left without seeing anyone else. As she stepped into the piazzetta Caprice came running after her.

'Jen,' Caprice caught up to her. Jen turned to look, and smiled in comfort. 'Can I take care of Marcello while you are out?' She reached out her arms. Jen paused with a moment of hesitation.

'Are you sure?'

'Si.'

Jen felt a bit relieved; it would be hard to look for a job with Marcello in her arms. 'Grazie.'

Marcello didn't seem to mind when he was passed over to Caprice. He smiled, and a little giggle could be heard. Jen kissed his forehead and smiled. It would be all right, Marcello told her.

It was late in the day by the time Jen left. And not knowing where she was off too, decided to be dropped off by the San Marco Piazza to wonder around. For an hour Jen did nothing but watch the Pigeons and the people, and compared the two. Because of the beautiful day, many people were out. It was already the beginning of October, which made Jen wonder what all these people were doing. *Don't they have to work?* A moment of doubt went through Jen as she thought about how she could get a job here. She spoke English, but her Italian needed work. She wouldn't even be able to speak Italian if she were lucky enough to get an interview.

And there Jen sat, at a Café in the middle of San Marco Piazza, wanting to cry, but no longer knowing how.

'Ma'am,' A waiter approached her. He came up slowly and she welcomed him. 'I have worked here many year, and I have never seen a face so… triste.' He lacked the word sad in his English vocabulary.

Jen could only smile back, however sad her smile appeared. And she wondered how Angelo would paint her if he saw her in this moment. Although the piazza was filled with people, no one sat at the café, letting the waiter see to Jen full time.

'You do not like here?' He asked.

Jen thought a moment before she replied. 'No, it is beautiful here.' She looked directly at him for the first time. 'My favorite place I have ever been too.'

'You fit here.' He smiled. Jen had been here long enough to realize that what he said was the largest compliment that you could receive in Venice.

'Grazie.' Jen had nothing else to say, so she bid him farewell and continued on with her day.

She was back to the beginning, she had been here since the end of June and she was right back where she started. She thought about Jerry, someone who left her trace of mind. Jerry had probably left, and was attending some university or college on a sports scholarship. She could picture him there, possibly a member of a fraternity with a beautiful girl at his side. The thought did nothing to her, she no longer cared for him the way that she thought she did. She didn't want to compare Angelo to Jerry, but she couldn't help it. Angelo was a man, and had a good twelve years on Jerry. He understood Jen, and helped her, and loved her, and was not embarrassed of her. For Jerry, Jen was just another check mark on his list. Jen diverted her attention to her father. She had called him only a handful of times, and most of the time she was talking to the voice mail that Jen had recorded a few months before she had left. She wondered if he missed her, she wondered if she needed him.

'Hello, dad?' She had made it through to him. She wanted to hear someone's voice. She had stopped by at a pay phone that seemed to be in the middle of no where.

'Hello.' He seemed happy and confused.

'How are you doing?'

'I miss you.' She wanted to cry, hearing him say that he missed her. For the first time in her life, she had been missed.

'I miss you too.'

'When are you coming home?'

She wanted to tell him everything, but she couldn't. Every time she tried, something stopped her. She wanted to tell him of her child, of Angelo and his family and where she actually was, but she couldn't.

'Hello, Jen?'

'Hi, dad. I'm still here.'

'When are you coming home?'

'I'm not sure, dad.'

'Well, I'm sorry I keep missing you when you call, I'm not home very much any more.' Pause. 'I got a job.'

'Really, dad? That's great.'

'Look, I have to go, but... I hope to see you soon.'

'Yeah.'

She sat listening to the beeping of the phone for a minute before she hung up. Slowly she replaced the phone on the receiver. This was the first time since she had left that she missed home. It was already October - she missed University, one of her dreams gone by.

Her thoughts shifted as she was reminded of the night before. Angelo knew what she had wanted, and made it what she needed. The thoughts became so strong she could feel his fingers upon her. She wished she could give back to Angelo what he gave to her, but she lacked the experience. How many woman has he had? Jen couldn't help but think. She wanted him to need her more than any other woman he had ever been with. Too much to ask for.

The best assimilation of the moment would be a slow motion close up of Jen's face, a song with a powerful moving beauty, and a thought. For feeling rather inverted and alone, as she walked through the streets, she was aware of everything around her. From the fast flow of humans walking by her to the steady movement of the water in the canals. She noticed the cracks on the streets and the warm breeze on her face. Before Jen knew it, she was lost, and the flow of people had dissipated. She was truly alone. She was alone with herself and her own noise. Each step clicking upon the stone was foreign to her. Being alone and lost didn't faze her, she just continued, lost in her own surroundings.

What led her further away was something least expected. A soft noise, almost child-like, a mystical laugh, the wandering echo. The misty face, covering the rock of illuminating life, vines and flowers covering the wall. In spite of everything Jen was going through, she smiled, *this is life,* she thought. No matter what, life is beautiful. She would get through this - everyone did.

That smile turned into a form of suspicion as she led herself to the beauty of the stone garden of a piazzetta which looked undiscovered. Towards the laughter.

The laughter that drew her in, the laughter that led her to where she was supposed to be... was laughter that didn't exist. It led her right into a trap, it risked her life, and left her alone. Abandoned her with herself. Something else appeared as she turned the corner into the piazzetta. Standing before her were three men. The men stood in a nook behind a brick wall, about three body length's away from her, and all could be clearly seen. The relationship between the three men was obvious. Jen paused, trying not to make a noise, and studied them. A transaction between, what looked like, life and death was going on. A pit formed at the bottom of Jen's stomach, it was as though she stood on a land mine - if she stepped off, or made a wrong move, she would die. Just like that.

Jen thought a moment, she couldn't chance it. She needed to get out of there. Just before she decided to move back, behind her the sound of a child's laughter rang between the narrow buildings as though the sound was trapped. Jen turned her head to see if this trick could be discovered. There was nothing there. She slowly turned her head back to where the three men stood. Now, however, one of them was staring directly at her.

Jen swallowed softly, and stepped back. She still watched and couldn't break from the gaze of this man. Suddenly a cluster of Italian words broke out from the other two men as they too noticed her. When Jen needed the strength everything seemed to fail her, her legs felt as though they turned into jelly. *Run , run damn it,* was all she could think.

The man who first noticed her pulled a gun from the inside pocket of his coat, and started heading towards her. At this point Jen bolted back to where she came from.

Heart racing, legs moving, thoughts yielding. She could see the road signs, up higher, painted on the corners of the buildings. Campo, Rio... everything meaning nothing to her. Pains jolted in her stomach, a pain she chose to ignore. Narrow street after narrow street, a man chasing her, no other soul around. Jen could feel her dress hike up past her thighs and felt the wind slam against her bare skin.

Suddenly it was night, the sun had set, and Jen was still being chased. Her lungs started to give up on her, and she could feel her throat turn scratchy and dry. The wind dried her tears. She came up to a place where she could go either way, it was almost crucial that she pick the right one. If she didn't, she could be stuck at a dead end. Without deciding she turned left and almost collided into a group of people. Quickly dodging them, her heart felt safe - there were other people. She turned back as she ran, there he was still chasing, a look as though he was ready to kill. His eyes caught hers again and she was locked.

Her step faltered, she tripped, her head hit... something... and her body slammed hard against the water.

Cool Pools

Chapter Five

I never thought that a little boy could grow so fast. I never thought that I could grow to love someone so much. Misty mornings, cool pools of water, sad thoughts filled my days, but he is always there. The change in me... to make me remember how fortunate I am.

His mother was an enchanting lady; music flowed through her veins as blood did to the rest of the human race. Her touch could not be compared. Marcello knew that my touch could never make up for his mother's. He still felt the tingle of her lips upon his forehead from the last time she had kissed him there, and he still tasted the saltiness of her tears. I would never fill that void. It was as though she was a goddess in a Roman myth. There was no way she could actually exist.

One day as I carried Marcello to the balcony and showed him the Gulf, I felt another presence in the room. Without looking, I thought I knew who it was but I was wrong. It was not Jen. I felt Angelo's arms gently hold me. I wondered if he thought I was her. Did he miss her? Did he know my feelings? I could not tell by the way he held me what he was thinking.

'Thank you, Kate.' He let go and stood beside me. My legs feeling light.

'I'm sorry?' Why was he thanking me?

'For everything you have done.' Angelo looked down at Marcello, who was now sleeping in my arms.

'It is my job.' I replied. Both him and I knew that was not actually the case.

Angelo smiled and walked away. What did he feel for her? He loves her, I could feel that much, I just wish that was not so. It was then that I realized she haunted him as much as she haunted me.

Jen spent the summer in France. From there she went to England, Germany and Spain. Instead of going home when the summer ended, she decided to finish her trip in Italy. And now it was the middle of October and she was stuck in the hospital. She had a private bedroom at the Ospedale Civile in Venice.

'I just wish that something would come back to me.' Jen laughed, trying to make light of the situation. She had been awake for only a few hours, and she was ready to lose all hope.

'Don't worry, I am sure one day it will come back to you, all of it, just like that.' He snapped his fingers. He looked at her as though he had known her for years. He looked at her with familiarity. Yet, she stared back at him vacant of any memory of hers with him in it. Although, when she looked into his eyes, she recognized something.

It was like the worst nightmare Jen could have. Ever since childhood, the thing that frightened her the most was forgetting. No longer remembering something that happened in her life. The thought of having forgotten something that, supposedly once, would make a life altering change was the unimaginable. As she grew up, she understood more and more. She knew she couldn't remember everything... but to lose a whole summer... it was too much.

Her head started to ache, and the pressure made her fall back into the coma she had just woken up from.

He had yet to truly hear her voice. Not even when she fell did she scream. It was as though when they locked eyes, he stole her voice. He stole her ability to scream for help. However, her eyes hid nothing and everything. Her eyes engraved in his mind, even though it was only a short time he had actually seen them.

He sat now at her bedside, waiting for her to wake up. Nervously holding his hands together, fiddling with his sweaty fingers.

She had already awoken once, and to Adam's benefit she could not remember who he was. Without thinking too much about it, he rambled on to her about the summer they had spent together. That was the only time he heard her voice, but he knew that it didn't actually come from her, it came from inside. She couldn't recall very much of anything, and seemed allusive. It was better that way. He didn't want to question her or prod her about what she remembered. It was his job to find out, but he would have to wait.

According to the hospital, they were engaged. It was the only way he could see her. If it was up to him, he would leave her, however there was no chancing what she knew.

Who would have guessed she didn't have traveler's insurance? Adam, without questioning, would be the one to pay for it.

'Mr. Salins, a word if you please.' He diverted his attention from Jennifer to the doctor, who stood at the door.

'Si.' Adam stood slowly.

'It seems that Jennifer has suffered a slight case of amnesia.' The doctor spoke a strong slow Italian.

'Slight?'

'Well, the only way we can truly find out is by asking her certain questions when she wakes up. We can only estimate that she has amnesia by the first time she woke. It is possible she will remember everything if she ever wakes up.'

'If?'

'By her brain activity we can only hope she will wake up.'

'Are you saying that she might always be in a coma?'

'Si.'

'But it was only a slip, a fall.'

'That is where you might be wrong, it seems that she always suffered some kind of seizure, but she has no records of epilepsy, so we can only assume.' The doctor paused but Adam couldn't speak. 'After a while we leave it up to you, if you want to keep her on support.'

Adam looked away. 'Grazie.' He resumed his position at the chair beside her bed. The hospital was leaving it up to him. He held the responsibility of this young woman in his hands. He watched her chest fill with air then empty. She was not even breathing for herself. When she slid back into the coma, it was as though she forgot to keep breathing. He could end it, right then. He could remove her breathing device and stop her life short. He closed his eyes for a moment. It would make his job easier, he wouldn't ever have to worry about her again. He stood now beside her bed, his hand resting upon her cheek. All you have to do is loosen it, no one will ever know.' It was hard for him to believe that he was actually talking himself into it.

He clutched the tube with his other hand a closed his eyes. *Pull damnit, just pull. You owe nothing to her.* Part of him wanted to leave this whole situation behind him. *Pull, just pull…*

As his shadow loomed over her, he became obsessed with another soul… these were no longer his thoughts.

'Did you want sponge her?' A nurse stepped into the room with a steaming bowl of soapy water and a few sponges. Adam almost stumbled; it took him a moment to find his voice. 'Yes… Si?' What was he agreeing to? He forced a smile.

'Grazie.' She smiled. Adam tried to hide his nervousness.

'Si.' Adam stood there dumbfounded. He was about to kill her, and now he was going to take care of her, clean her. Emotions flying around. *Hopefully the nurse had not noticed anything unusual,* was all he could think. He placed the basin on the table beside her bed, placing the sponge cautiously into the water. It steamed, as did his hand. He watched the water evaporate off his hand and lingered in the sensation. He wondered if, in her sleep, whether or not she could feel the touch of the wet sponge and the water and of his hand, perhaps in dream.

Looking at her, he didn't know where to begin. It was only in this moment did he see her as something more than a problem. She was a human. Softly sleeping, not knowing but trusting that someone in this harsh world would take care of her. Suddenly he was the one that wanted to take care of her. He wanted to make sure that she would be all right. He touched her soft skin with the sponge and watched as the water poured slowly off the curves of her body, taking all the moisture her skin needed.

Only one thing made sense and even that left a pit at the bottom of his stomach. Only one thing felt real; the reaction of her skin beneath his, the tingling in his spine as he washed her - the feeling of life. Of life.

This is when it could have happened. This could have been the very moment where Adam fell in love with Jen. Maybe not falling in love with her, but the idea of her. Falling in love with how this moment made him feel. How easily one hates and how easily one loves. Nevertheless, how lame he felt was masked, as love has no explanation. If someone had asked him, he would tell everyone it was when the two of them were in Brighten, England, even though Jen had no recollection of it. Jen would have to spend the time falling in love with him again, being told of the lost and forgotten moments.

***

'Is she?'

'No… she has yet to really wake up.'

'Dammit, Adam…' He hit the wall hard. 'You know what they will do to you if you don't follow through.'

'You think I don't know that?' Adam's voice didn't even rise in the slightest. He was calm and collected, maybe that was why he was so good at his job.

'They would do to us, to US, Adam?'

'Tom, I know.'

'So why don't you do it?'

Adam looked out of the window to a canal that he had yet to see anyone pass through. So cracked and old, left abandoned.

'I can't.' He flinched.

'This is not the Adam I know. She is in the way of millions of dollars, in the way of our lives. It could so easily be a mistake.'

'No…' Adam snarled. It was his obligation to take care of her. She trusted him, it was in her sleep, in sleep. She trusted him for a moment, when she woke, with her eyes. 'What I mean to say is… there is a hope… she has a case of amnesia.'

'How can we prove it to them? What about her family, people will be looking for her, have you not thought about that?'

'We have a hospital report, she doesn't even have an identity. Trust me.'

Tom sat at the edge of the hotels bed, letting out a huge sigh. His elbows on his knees and his hands running through his greasy hair. 'Fuck.'

Adam searched his pockets and pulled out a package of cigarettes, without thinking, took one and tossed the package to Tom. 'Fine, Tom, if you think you could do it… you go to the hospital.'

'Maybe I will.' Tom stood as he lit his cigarette.

Without understanding why, Adam put on his defense. And this was against his best man. He put on a defense against a guy that, more than once, saved his life.

'It's like she has you under some kind of spell…fuck.'

Adam tensed. It was probably true.

***

'Do it.' Adam placed his hand on Toms shoulder. Tom, lost in the very existence of Jen, he didn't even seem to notice Adam beside him. Adam laughed and walked beside the hospital bed. He didn't even notice that his hand had made it to her cheek, but he found it there, in comfort.

'This is insane.' Tom finally broke his trance. 'What are we going to do?'

'I will take her back home.'

'Where is that?'

'I'm not sure. I will find out and I will take her away.'

'Adam, in three days we are suppose to meet in Egypt.' Tom turned unable to hold his anger. 'I'm not going by myself.'

'Then we opt this one out.'

'Not possible. This could be our biggest break ever.'

Adam looked at her… she slept. No sign of waking up any time soon. He was willing to give up the possibility of millions of dollars for a woman he hardly knew.

'We will make it work.'

'Don't say that. Stop saying that.'

'You watch over her and take her home when she wakes up. I go to Egypt.'

'By yourself?' Tom couldn't believe this.

'Yes.'

No words came out of Tom's mouth, he just shook his head and watched Jen.

'When she wakes up, you take her home.' Adam slid his hand into hers. 'Tell her I will meet her. Keep me informed. Buy her a ticket home, wait with her until I get back. We still split the job. Okay? We still split the job.' It was not a question.

'Adam, I…'

'Please.'

Silence. With every second that Tom said nothing took away an ounce of hope for Adam.

'I have no other choice. If we want her to live, we have no other choice.'

'Thank you.'

'I'm not doing it for you. I'm – I'm doing it for her.'

Adam looked at Tom, and for a moment wished he was staying, he could see Tom was already lost under her spell. Whatever the spell was.

Three days later Adam took off on a plane to Egypt, not realizing it would be four months before he would be able to see her again. Tom spent a moment everyday to see her. He wouldn't allow himself to stay very long, only a few moments. And when no one else was in the room he would read out loud as though she could hear the daily news and, most importantly, a daily insight of Rumi. Then before leaving, a sigh, a savored moment, and out the door, trying not to look back.

But the third day after Adam had left, he began to notice something unusual. Something almost embarrassing. On her hospital gown were two wet spots which came from her breasts, as though she was a nursing mother. Without ever notifying anyone, he covered her, cursed, and left the room. Nothing ever came of it. No doctor ever said anything, and it never happened again. It was only lost in Tom's mind.

The day that Jen woke up was a surprise to everyone at the hospital. The longer it takes for someone in a coma to wake up, the less the chances are that they ever will open their eyes again.

And Tom did his job. He sat there beside her bed, waiting… reading… waiting. And when she woke up, after two weeks of being immobile, she woke from some dream, nightmare, or lost world. Lying flat with I.V.'s draining into her and bright lights that blinded her vision, and she still did nothing to move. Too unsure… too afraid she couldn't.

When she woke up it took her over an hour before she spoke. Noticing Tom but too afraid to ask him who he was, knowing that she should know him. No one noticing for the hour that she was awake.

Oddly enough she recognized it, the old hospital. Something vaguely familiar left her wondering. She had just woke up… maybe a few hours before, or was it already the next day? That's all she remembered. She woke up to a pair of eyes that haunted her even now. A man that she had just spent the summer traveling around Europe with. A man she was supposed to remember.

Jen spent that time before anyone saw her trying to recollect her last memory. Nothing of Europe came back to her. She knew she could try to start with 'hello', and get to know him and remember. At least there would be pictures.

What was the last thing Jen remembered? A memory recently in her mind was... Jerry. It made her smile, Jerry. She missed him. But what happened to him? *Why isn't he with me? Why isn't his hand in mine?*

She would have to get home soon, finish her last year of high school, get her diploma, and go to University. But who was this man she woke up to the first time? She recognized his eyes, but from where? And where was he now?

The man that sat beside her, reading didn't look at all familiar. His silhouetted side view was all she could see. Her eyes could not focus properly; the light in the room washed him away. He was not looking at her, he, too, was lost from this world.

Frustration blinded her with tears. Home wasn't close enough. She had no recollection of the time or space around her. No recollection of the year, the month, how much of her life was lost, her age. Had she finished school? Everything felt so overwhelming, even the taste of her salty tears.

Her throat blocked up, her breathing became labored, she couldn't tell if was possible for her to even move her body. A part of her began to think she had become paralyzed. *What happened to me? Why am I so confused. Is everyone okay?* It took Jen a few minutes before she built up enough courage to slightly lift her legs. With much effort, they moved with no physical restrictions. She smiled, relief, she could naturally again. A small giggle was released from her lips, unsure of whether the sound came from her or not.

That is when the silhouette stranger turned to her. His eyes filled with extreme surprise, smiling with happiness, unsure of how he was supposed to feel. They locked eyes onto each others, silence seemed to overwhelm them. Jen needed the moment to find this man in her memory, but it never happened. Before this stranger could speak, Jen took the opportunity.

'I know that I am supposed to know you... but I am sorry, I don't.' He could see the tears well up in her beautiful crystal eyes. 'I will try, maybe one day it will...'

His slight laughter interrupted her apologizes. 'Don't, you don't know me, and your not supposed to know me.' He came closer, he was no longer the silhouetted figure.

'I don't know you?'

'No.'

'Why are you here then?'

Tom smiled. Jen noticed how nice his smile was, how comforting, but was still unsure of what was going on. Before Tom could say 'I don't know,' his impulses stopped him. 'I am here on Adam's behalf, your fiancé?' *Will she remember? Does she know everything, anything? God, Adam why do you put me in these situations? What do I do if she remembers being chased?*

'Right… is Adam okay?' Genuine concern washed over her face, which made Tom wonder how she could care for someone she actually didn't know. 'I miss him.'

'You do?' This was all too bizarre.

'Yeah, I think so.'

'What do you miss about him?' He was trying not to play with her, but the situation seemed so unreal.

'I'm not sure…' Silence. 'His eyes haunt mine. I feel them on me.' Staring off. 'I miss the memories, I'm sure one day…' Her voice trailed off. She almost had to force something out of her throat, it felt hoarse and sounded foreign to her.

Tom couldn't figure out what to say, he wanted to comfort her, but didn't feel that it was his right. He wanted to say something, but didn't know what. He wanted to kiss her on the forehead and hold her, and tell her to forget about Adam. *Shit. She lay there so vulnerable to his presence, her heart willing to trust and accept anything I have to say.*

The longest silence. Silence that could slice through anything was broken by a nurse quietly walking into the room.

'She is awake, si.' She stopped, her eyes widened and smiled as though it was her own child that was laying in front of her. The nurse placed down the basin of hot water by her bed and put her hands in Jen's.

Jen slightly laughed, overwhelmed by this, waking up. A bolt of energy quickly came back to her. She felt restricted by the hospital bed, but tried to sit up for the first time anyway. The nurse changed the position of the bed, so that Jen could sit up without effort.

'You do not want to move so much, you must build strength over time.'

'Grazie.' Jen spoke as the nurse helped her through. *Where did that come from? I am so lost.* She knew she was in a hospital in Italy, but where were these Italian words coming from?

'Come state facendo?' *How are you doing?*

'Buon.' The nurse laughed.

'I just did not realize that I had those words in me.' Waking up to this new world scared Jen. It was hard to take. Everything in her recent memory seemed to be ancient history. Where were Jerry and her friends, her dad, and her job at the Diner? Italian? If she couldn't remember anything that happened in Italy, how could she remember Italian? Her head started to hurt, and her throat seemed to clog up again.

Without realizing that the nurse had left, and that Tom had replaced his hands with hers, Jen continued to wonder.

'This life is so confusing. I need to remember, my mind feels as though it were a million different pieces.'

'It will come back, memories and moments will return to you.' Tom looked out at the window when he said that, wanting to comfort her, but worried that everything might come back, and she would remember who Adam actually was. 'What is the last thing that you remember?'

'I ... mountains, the Rocky Mountains with my boyfriend...' She closed her eyes. 'Sorry... with the person I remember as my boyfriend. I am lost. What time, day, month, year... what is all of this? That memory could be from years ago. Where am I?'

Tom never realized that the date and time could be so important to someone, but upon telling Jen everything, he was proven wrong. The last thing she remembered was the summer before entering her last year of high school, which meant her last memory had to be over one year and three months ago. Tom couldn't imagine what it would be like to have a chunk of his life missing from his mind, it would be hard to deal with.

Tom spent his time away from the hospital doing his research, always a part of the job. Jennifer Ann Sipi. He found her age, her father, the fact that her mother had died in childbirth. He found where Jen was from - a small town near the Rocky Mountains in Canada. He contacted the Canadian Embassy and reported the accident, and there was no recovery of her passport. The last thing that Tom tried to do was call her father, who, he imagined, would be quite worried about his daughter. But upon calling it only resulted in leaving a message.

How easily all of this happened. Adam had told him that the reason why she lapsed into such a coma was that upon falling, she had suffered some sort of seizure. There were no records of having any sort of epilepsy, but this sort of thing was more common than unheard of. Unusually enough, upon scanning her doctor files, there was a record of her being pregnant. But the dates didn't add up, and there was no record of her even having the child. She must have miscarried, which would make sense as why she started to lactate. Maybe it was a good thing she didn't remember all that, it could break her heart to know.

'How does it feel?' Tom finally got the courage to ask. 'How does it really feel... not to remember?'

She took a moment before she answered, closing her eyes. 'Imagine going to sleep in your room... recalling the day... the people in your life... listing off in your mind before you fell asleep what you needed to do the next day... and possibly smiling before you drift off into another realm... possibly dreaming, then you wake up in a nightmare... everything you thought you knew, you didn't. Where were the people in your life? They just disappeared. Where were they to help me? Lost. I am so lost. Engaged to a different man, a man I am sure is great. I feel like I let him down, I can't even remember him, how could he ever forgive me? How can I forgive myself? Not only do I wake up in a hospital, but a hospital that is somehow placed on the other side of the world. But the worst part, I am not sure how I got from point A to point B. I am wondering when I am going to wake up. I have had two birthdays since I can last remember. I am so disorientated. It is like getting lost in a foreign country and never finding your way out. At least I remember my birthday: November 4th. I think. Fuck. I am so gone. I feel so broken and destroyed. I just want to wake up from this nightmare.' *Stop. Breathe. Open your eyes.* She looked at this stranger in her life, a tear was forming at the bottom of his eyes. He had followed the path she described, and, with her words, left the pain to this new stranger in her life. 'I am sorry…' they caught each others eyes. '… thanks… I don't even know you, it has been the only consoling thing I have had in this nightmare.'

'Don't apologize, please, I needed to understand, and now I do.' *I'm not good in these situations. Dammit, Adam, where are you?* He hadn't heard from Adam in over a week and there was no way of reaching him on his end. For all Tom knew, Adam could have stopped breathing a week ago. *Shit, I should have known this. How many times has Adam needed me in the past? I should have known that he couldn't handle it on his own.* Toms palms started sweating, and his nerves started taking over.

'You look like you have been through more than I have.' Jen slightly laughed. 'Are you feeling alright?' Tom nodded. 'Good, because I would like to stand. Jen removed the blankets from her legs and tried to slowly get up.

Tom was at her side in seconds. 'No… please wait for the nurse.'

'I know, I know.'

Within minutes, Tom tracked down a nurse and Jen had the chance to walk. The nurse brought into the room a walking bar and another nurse, so they could both help her out of bed. Wow, this is a big deal. It had only been two months, truly it won't be that hard. Before the nurses let Jen walk they called on the doctor, who had seen her every couple hours since she had woke up.

'Glad to see that you are doing good.' The doctor seemed as though he was animated, almost cartoon like.

Jen couldn't help but release a giggle. 'Si, Grazie. Non ha potuto ritenere piu megilo.' Couldn't feel better.

'Very good, I did not even know that you could speak Italian.'

'Either did I.'

Everyone in the room seemed surprised; Tom didn't know what to think. If she could remember Italian, maybe everything was coming back to her. What if she remembered?

Her first attempt at walking was harder then she could have ever thought. Within moments she fell, only to be caught by the nurses. The two nurses stayed by her side with each step. By the time she made it to the end of the bar, she was too tired to go back. She didn't have to ask, the nurses knew, without being told that it was time for her to rest.

When everyone left the room, Jen took a moment to examine her body. Although she felt frail, she noticed changes that didn't seem to make sense. She missed all this growing, she looked more like a woman than she ever had before. Her curves more succulent than she ever remembered, her breasts full and beautiful. Jen liked her body, but missed the transformation, and wondered when that had happened.

***

Tom didn't understand it, nor did he think he ever would, but the weeks passed by him like water running through his fingers. He stayed by Jen's side, going through with her the pain she suffered everyday. It was a new experience for him, everyday he walked into her room he learned more of her, and realized that he knew more about herself then she did. He didn't understand it, but he truly began to care for her. In which way, he did not know. His feelings went past understanding, his feelings left him lost and confused. He had almost forgotten about Adam when he was around her, but he couldn't help but worry. He had still not heard from Adam, leaving Tom lost on what to do. He knew he had to keep on this job, he couldn't just abandon Jen and look for Adam in Egypt. He couldn't contact the American Embassy, Adam was in Egypt under the law. He was only left to worry and pray.

When the time came for Jen to go home, he took her from the hospital to his place in Venice. As they left he could do nothing else but watch her. As he had come in and out of these doors and traveled this path twice a day for the last couple months, this was Jens first time. If she had experienced this before, she showed no signs of it.

'We go home tomorrow.' Tom stated as they reached his place. ' I'm sorry for the mess, I didn't expect you to see this place.'

He watched her look out the window as he prepared for her a chilled glass of Italian wine. She looked as though she were lost in a nostalgic thought as he approached her with the glass of wine. He stood too close. There was a tear in her eye, but getting to know her, he knew that she would never admit to it. 'I need to go home.'

'Okay.' Tom stood behind her, and felt her back against his chest. He was somber and wondered how this came to be. Everyday he was with Jen she always mentioned Adam. However this night, at this moment, there was no mention of him. Only a memory.

Midnight Television

Chapter Six

Venice is a small city, I once heard a fact that you can fit all of Venice inside of Hyde Park in London; only six hundred thousand people inhabit this place. For a city, that number reads small, but for a city as small as Venice the amount of people is quite vast. Everyday, however, someone runs into someone they know. There is no hiding, ever. A smile, a laugh and move on to follow the day's path. But for some reason no one ran into Jen, which means that Jen also never ran into anyone. And as Jen went home, I was none the wiser. I watched the sky that day and saw the plane up in the sky. Never thinking that she would be on it. I held little Marcello and pointed up into the sky. 'Aereo' I said, his response was a giggle. No sign of his mother coming home, coming back.

It had been sometime since we had last seen Jen. Her possessions were left here, not a single thing had been touched since she left. There was something wrong, she couldn't have just left knowingly. I held Marcello unable to breast feed him, unable to stop his tears, cursing the name of his mother, wondering how any mother could ever abandon her child.

As I walked inside that day the place seemed darker than usual. A looming figure stood in the hallway, a figure I knew too well.

'Angelo?' There was no response. A moment of silence broken by the sound of a child. Angelo turned towards me, and I saw his pain. I saw what she did to him.

'She will be back.' Angelo stiffened in some sort of defense. 'There is no way she left.'

'I am sorry.' I responded. I could not comfort him, there was no way. I wish I could have hugged him, or pressed my lips to his, and told him she was not worth it. But that would be a lie, because all of me knew that she was.

Angelo turned from me as though he was about to leave and then turned back. 'May I?' He reached out his arms for Marcello. I handed him the child, and, although Marcello was not Angelo's, he treated him as if he was. And unless Angelo in future years ever told him the difference, Marcello could never know.

I wanted to make everything better - touch him and melt away the pain, but there seemed no way. Angelo seemed tired, his face grew dark and aged, his eyes seemed crazed. And all I could do was curse the name of Marcello's mother for causing so much pain. Angelo had spent the first week of her disappearance at the Police station, sure that she had been kidnapped or hurt or worse yet murdered. But none of it made sense; it was all helpless. He had no evidence of her true existence, without true identification they came up empty handed.

Afterward, he posted pictures of her face he had so vividly sketched and filed her as a missing person. But now it had almost been three months since she went missing and even a small sign.

It was about time everyone moved on. It was about time. However, with her child left behind there was no way they could forget her, and there was no way anyone would let the child go.

Angelo seemed to disappear everyday lost in his mind. I always wondered how much someone was capable of loving another. I saw it, he could not stop loving her, wherever she was, whoever she was. Even it if was the last memory of her. Would there ever be closure? This family needed one, I needed one. And if Jen was alive she would know no difference.

As the years passed, her memory did not fade from this home. Hope was lost, all but the slightest ounce. And as the boy grew the features of his mother flared out on him. Marcello, too young to know but wise enough to realize I was not his mother.

Tom stayed with Jen and took her home, just as he promised Adam. The festive season just passed, but the remnants still left hanging in the air. As the two stepped onto the land, just outside the airport, Jen smiled, this is something she knew. Some sort of pressure was released from her.

'Yes, I know this place.' She smiled with her arms outstretched. There was this small fear inside her that all of this would be unrecognizable, but that disappeared. She could never forget this.

'Home.' Tom stated.

'Oh no, not yet.' They took an hour and a half shuttle down the highway and into the Rocky Mountains. Tom had never seen this world wonder before, and didn't notice the time passing as he stared out the window lost in natural beauty. Never had Tom thought that it would be this amazing. Yes, he had seen pictures, but pictures never did this feeling justice. Jen noticed the boyish look Tom had on his face as they drove further into the mountains. He didn't notice the civilization around, he seemed to ignore it.

'Jen?' She turned her head smiling to recognize her father waiting at the open door of the house.

'Dad.' Suddenly dropping every thought, she ran across the small lawn to his arms. Something felt different from the memory she had of him, he looked the same, perhaps a little aged, but the difference was cupped in a small vibe that he gave off.

'Dad, you look great.' She couldn't describe it. It had been over half a year since she had seen her father. Most of the time he had been oblivious to the fact that she had been living in Venice. Jen tried to recall her last memory of him, but he was too different.

Tom had been able to get a hold of her father. Before they came back, he described her condition and filled him in with what had happened. Jen would never remember telling her father that she was away for the summer with a friend, rather than across the world. Even still her father welcomed them home, giving Tom the spare room, which was actually the living room. The comfort of midnight television.

They had only been sitting and comfortable for five minutes when Jen's father stopped and asked the question; 'Why didn't you tell me you were going to Italy?'

Jen's face turned white as her attention focused to her father, 'What?'

'I never knew…' a slight hesitation. 'I never knew that you went to Italy, when you left you mentioned you were going to spend the summer with a friend… I can't remember her name.'

'No I didn't, did I?' She really didn't know, how could she remember. Tom wanted to defend her, defend her condition, but nothing would come. His impulses told him to stay away.

'Dad, I…' She struggled not to cry. 'I don't know.' Jen stood and looked away, as though she was trying to calm down or remember. 'Dad, I can't remember when I left, or why I left… I can't remember graduating or turning eighteen, or nineteen for that matter. I don't remember changing my room to that. I remember Jerry…' a small laugh, '… for all I know I am still dating him. Dad… I know that this is no excuse, but all I can do, all I can say, is I'm sorry.'

Jen walked away and didn't turn back. That night she stayed in her room and stared at posters she never even remembered putting up.

It seemed like hours had passed before Tom could even look at her father, who sat at the kitchen table, and silently cried. Before Tom could say or do anything they both heard a scream of anger come from Jen's room. Both men stood, they looked at each other. Without a word Mr. Sipi indicated that Tom should be the one to check on her. The tension in the house was too much. The misunderstandings, the pain, the unresolved feelings floated around, enough to suffocate any one.

After a slight knock on her door and no response, Tom entered her small room. The posters that once covered the walls of her room were ripped to the floor and Jen curled in a ball at the opposite corner of the door, let out a small weep of failure. Too many tears she had cried. Tom's lack of words, all he could do was hold her, all night, until she lost herself in sleep.

No one ever mentioned that night again. But Tom spent years after thinking about it, wishing he could do… something.

***

'Well, I don't know.' Her voice honest and calm. There was no quiver of fear or loss triggering in her voice, however this completely contradicted her words.

'Oh…Oh.' No one could think of anything to say. Tom only watched. He really wanted to laugh, as he wondered how Jen turned out so much different from her high school friends. They sat at a small local diner, Jen trying to remember if she was still on the payroll or not. No one that worked there looked the same, and if she was supposed to know them, they made no reference on knowing her. Jen decided she wanted to check out the place, check if she still remembered it, but as they decided to leave a group the high school friends Jen knew walked in, leading to this truly awkward conversation that was dealt out in front of them now. She was bombarded with a thousand and one questions, which led Jen into explaining what happened to her to the best of her knowledge.

'So I can't believe you traveled Europe, what was your favorite place?' One of her friends asked.

'Well,' Jen rolled her eyes in Tom's direction. They both wanted to laugh, but stayed straight faced. 'Well, I don't know.'

There were three of them that kept asking her questions. All good friends, but Jen couldn't understand them. *Had they all changed? Was I like this once? When did Sarah cut her hair like that? How did Tracy lose all that weight? And when the hell did Kyle start hanging out with Sarah and Tracy? I am sure he once said he hated them more than anything.* All these questions and thoughts forced themselves into Jens mind, making her want to scream. She knew she just couldn't come out and ask, but these were the things she wanted to know the moment they walked in. *I'm not ready for this.*

'But you're engaged?' Kyle asked in bewilderment.

'I think so.' Jen looked over at Tom for help, but he had nothing to say. 'We met in Europe, I guess, we traveled together for a few months and in Brighten, England, he asked me to marry him?' Her voice was so unsure. This was only the second time she had repeated the story, it was still foreign to her.

'Was it romantic?' Tracy just didn't get it.

'Yeah, I imagine it was.' Tom tried not to laugh as Jen spoke, wandering off into a day dream. 'I imagine any man like Adam would have to be romantic.'

Tom almost broke right there and told her everything. As much as he missed Adam, he wanted to hit him. Did Adam understand the consequences he put the both of them in?

'Well, were is Adam right now?' Sarah asked.

'He is in Egypt, working... he will be here shortly.' Jen felt like she had to defend herself from all these questions. She never told Tom her worries. If Adam loved her so much, why hadn't he called her, told her anything? None of Adam's absence made any sense.

'So Tom, have you ever been to Canada before?' Kyle asked. He seemed smarter then the rest and stopped bombarding Jen with questions that only made her look more distressed. Easily enough he changed the topic.

'No, this is my first time. It is beautiful here. Everyone always sees pictures, but they are nothing compared to the feeling of actually being here. Must admit it is extremely cold here.'

' You came at a bad time, middle of winter is cold everywhere. In the summer it gets really nice though. Hopefully you will come back in the summer some day.' Kyle drank his beer.

'Yeah, I missed the mountains. You sometimes forget how beautiful they are when you have lived here for so long. But there is something so comforting here.' Jen still seemed distant from everyone. 'Come on, Tom, let's go.' She stood and grabbed Tom's arm.

She never looked back, but Tom did. Her friends sat in confusion. What could they say to stop her? Things had changed.

As the two of them walked into the cool refreshing air of the night, there was a long silence. Both thinking of what next to say, both too frightened to say it. Finally, when they both came up with enough courage to say something, they started tripping over each other's words.

'Sorry, you go first.' Jen laughed.

'No you go.'

'It's just that it's not the same, nothing is.'

'I know.'

'I can't be in there.' She looked over her shoulder and back to the small diner. 'They... I don't know them anymore, they are different.'

'So are you.' Were Tom's only words.

'I know, I know. It's just that... I don't want to be here, maybe that's why I left in the first place.'

Tom knew what she was getting at, but kept silent; he didn't know how to answer. 'Ahh..' was all he could say.

'I have to see him.' Jen stopped walking, and took a serious long look at Tom. No wondering, no tomorrows, no reasons, no excuses. 'Where is he? Why hasn't he talked to me? I know what this is.'

Tom froze. For a moment Tom thought he had been caught. He thought that she knew what they did for work, and that Adam was actually missing… somewhere.

'What is this?' He spoke softly.

'I think Adam is scared. I think that he ran from me. He didn't know what to do.' She started walking again, faster this time. 'I don't blame him. I hate myself for not remembering who I am, who Adam is. But I need to face it. You know where he is, stop hiding him from me. There is something missing from this puzzle.'

Tom had problems keeping up to her pace, and the more he denied anything the faster she would walk.

'Look… Adam is not scared, he loves you more than anything… its just that work is keeping him busy, and he wants to give you time.'

STOP. TURN. A SHARP LOOK. 'That's bullshit, Tom. I know it is.' *Turn away, keep walking.*

'Look, Jen. Please. I don't know where he is.' Tom called out, not being able to keep up to her. That stopped Jen dead in her tracks, but she didn't look at him, stood staring in the dark abyss, a street that seemed to disappear into the night. ' Jen…' Tom walked closer. 'I'm sorry. We were keeping in touch, but I lost contact with him, a few weeks ago. He is in Egypt somewhere… I'm going to find him.' *Fuck, don't tell her too much.*

Tom wondered what would make her turn around, but nothing seemed to work. By the time he finished speaking, he stood right behind her. Without thinking, and only out of comfort he placed his hand gently on her shoulder. She turned to him quickly, not hiding the tears. The tears she didn't feel, the tears she never knew she had.

Something attracted Jen to Tom, in this moment, a new memory. Jen came in and held him. And this time without thinking, Jen looked up to him and placed her lips on his. What Tom should have done was stop, move away and pull back. That is what he should have done. But he didn't move. He locked lips with her and melted into her arms. Not thinking of the consequences, only knowing that he felt something for her, and didn't care about anything else. Lost minds, distorted views and found lips.

'Shit.' Jen stopped mid kiss and pushed herself away. Her eyes looked down and her hair poured in front of her face. Her lips still full and wet from their kiss. There was nothing said for a while. The silence of the night, melding only into a distant language. 'I'm sorry.'

'No, I am sorry.'

There was no reason to be sorry for this kiss. Yes perhaps other reasons, for lying about this woman's life, for falling for her considering her loyalties fall with Adam, a man she actually didn't know. But Jen should not be the one saying sorry. *I can't live with this lie any more.*

'You must think that I'm this… some kind of slut.' She stepped back. She continued to look down as though she were ashamed. ' I need to be by myself.' She took off walking down a different street. Tom only watched her walk away. He knew nothing of this place, this mysterious mark on the map. The only direction he knew was two blocks straight forward and a block to the left he would be able to stand right in front of her house. Something felt wrong to go back to her house at this time, so her turned back around and went in the direction of the diner.

It was only a moment ago that he kissed her. He would be lying if he didn't admit that he would have kissed her the moment she woke up, but he didn't.

Tom stepped back into the diner, only this time it was empty. *Damn Adam, damn the lies and damn this situation.*

'Hi, can I get something for you?' The server approached him with a recognizable smile.

'Yeah, whiskey on the rocks.'

'Right up.' She mixed the drink and handed it to him. 'Hope it works.' Tom couldn't bother to ask what she meant, he assumed she meant the drink, but of course it meant the girl, it always means the girl.

Time must have passed, nothing but the feeling of warm whiskey going down his throat indicated the passing of time. What did time mean to people? Nothing but the measure of the passing moment. Nothing but the revolving of the sun east to west. Nothing but the lapping of water at a door step. It becomes hard to settle when you feel responsible for someone who is missing, or you fall in love with someone you can't have.

Tom felt it hard to believe that he made it from his warm spot in the diner to a path that led him to this mysterious lake. *Did I even pay my tab? Shit.*

'God, it is beautiful here.' He said out loud to only himself, and God if he was listening. It was dark, but distant lights glazed upon the calm water, partly frozen, partly not. It was silent, aside from the distant partiers and the lapping of water on the rocks and ice. The path led both ways around the lake, and Tom didn't know which way to go, so he sat on a rock close enough to the water that he could put his feet on. The cold from the rock made him jump up and decide against sitting. He could see his breath dispersing into the midnight air. He hadn't been outside long enough to know how cold it was until now.

When he decided it was time to walk back to the house… wherever it was, he started to hear the group of partiers screaming to someone. The splashing of water indicated that someone had jumped into the lake. Stupid kids, he thought as he meant to walk away. It was the call of a certain name being called that stopped him.

'JEN, get back here, come on.' Upon hearing that, he couldn't walk away, he had to make sure, he had to check, if it was his Jen. He rushed to where he heard the voices and recognized a few of Jen's friends as they noticed him.

'What is she doing?' He asked her friends, ready to snap at one of them.

'She was drinking... no one could stop her.'

'Shit.' Tom started toward Jen who seemed a great distance in the water. There she was dancing in the frigid water, singing, falling, laughing.

'Jen.' Tom shouted. 'Come back here.'

'Tom?' Jen screamed back, 'is that you?' A laugh, a trip, a fall, another laugh. 'Come in the water, its just right.' She started spinning with her arms up to the stars. 'Look at the stars... Tom... look.'

He could see her only from the reflection of the fire on the side of the lake. He was close enough to shore to notice the outline of her body was nothing but her's, no clothes to obstruct the silhouette of her curves.

'What happened to her clothes?' Tom didn't want to get angry at anyone, but he couldn't help but sound completely annoyed. 'Jen come back here please.'

'No Tom... it's too nice here.'

Tom didn't like his solution but it was the only one he could think of. He took off his jacket and headed into the water. He needed to get her out. Shit, the water is cold. He couldn't understand how Jen could feel fine in the water with no clothes on. 'Jen come back. He started kicking the water as he walked further out.

'So you decided to join me?' She laughed, no signs of being embarrassed.

'Jen, please come here.'

'Let's stay out here and look at the stars.' She shouted. *Why was she being so stubborn?* Tom tried to ignore how beautiful she looked, like the Goddess of the water. The reflection of light on her skin, and her hair blowing in the wind. He more than lusted for her, her body full and beautiful, but he tried to look away.

As he reached her, he put his arms around her and covered her with his arms. 'Come on, let's go back.' She looked at him naked, with no shame.

'Hi, do you like the water?' She laughed.

'Let's go back.'

'Okay.'

'Can someone get some towels or blankets?' Tom shouted back to the shore. That's when he noticed that everyone was watching as they came out from the water, no single eyes diverted. Tom did the most respectful thing he could do. Although freezing he took off his mostly dry t-shirt and covered Jen with it. He couldn't stand everyone watching her naked. A couple people ran to meet him at the shore with a couple blankets. Tom covered her and started rubbing her shoulders and back to create friction and heat.

'Come, I will drive you both home.' Kyle said from the crowd.

'Kay.' Jen responded before Tom could. Tom wanted to seek some form of medical attention. In his days before Adam, he worked for Emergency Medical Services, before he turned into this being. Money had too much influence.

Tom scooped her up into his arms and followed Kyle. In less then ten minutes they were parked in front of Jen's tiny home and lifting her to the door. Tom thanked Kyle and carried Jen to the couch. There was no one home, and Tom only wondered for a moment where Mr.Sipi was, but the heavy shivering that came from Jen halted those thoughts.

'Jen?' He noticed her lack of circulation, her skin turning blue. Tom sat next to her and started rubbing her again to keep her warm. After a while, it looked like the warm fire of her tears melted the blue color away around her face.

'I can't feel my fingers.' She acted as though she was just a small child. But Tom didn't care.

'What happened Jen?,' he said as he took off the wet t-shirt and cold blanket she was wearing. Quickly he covered her up with a warm dry blanket. Without thinking he too stripped down out of his wet clothing, and covered himself in another dry blanket.

At first he didn't notice Jen's widened eyes, but as he did a smirk covered his face, and she blushed.

'I only left you, I didn't figure you would try to hurt yourself.'

'I didn't.' She tried to defend, her voice still slurred from her over indulgence in some sort of alcoholic beverage.

'I thought the lakes up here freeze solid.' Tom said more to himself. ' I have never been in any water that cold in my life.'

'That one doesn't, it's too deep.' Jen couldn't even look at him. Finally she felt ashamed, sitting crunched up on the corner of the couch shivering.

'What were you thinking?'

'I wasn't, okay! I'm sorry.'

Tom took the silence of the moment to sit down beside her.

'No Jen, I'm sorry. You scared me, that's all. If you were in that water any longer you could have died.' He couldn't even look at her. He could only think about what would have happened had he not been there. He thought of the kiss he wished he could finish, he thought about her cold body next to his. But then he thought about Adam.

'Jen?' He waited for her to look at him, 'I have to go.'

She looked away before she could answer, 'I know.'

'Is there anything...'

'Yes,' Jen smiled sadly. 'You could tell him, I miss him. I think.' She spoke through her shivering. Nothing else was said that night, not even a 'good night,' as she drifted off into sleep. The next morning Tom left Jen, alone on the couch, wondering if he was ever going to see her again. He packed his few things and bought a one way ticket to Egypt. It was time for him to start looking for his friend. He knew that he would spend the plane trip trying not to think about her, yet she was the only entity that consumed his mind. And as his plane took off he wondered if it was true the advice his mother once gave him. *If you are thinking of a person, it is because they are thinking of you.* Part of him wanted to believe his mother was right, but he knew that Jen was too lost to think of him. He could tell from miles away that she was a lost soul. Lost even before the accident, and all he wanted to do was help her find it. Finding it, however, was not his job.

***

'You drive,' she said as she hugged up behind him. He didn't even worry about his helmet as he straddled the bike and flew across the long straight road of the sandy desert. He flipped into the highest gear as he prayed he would get away.

Adam didn't have an easy stay stop over in Egypt. The last few months that he hoped to bury behind him were not up to the standard of living. He was locked in a small prison cell, meant only for a large dog, but made of half inch thick iron bars. He had absolutely no contact with anyone from the outside world. But it didn't stop him from constantly thinking about his escape. Once he did figure out how to escape from his dog cage, what would he do? After escaping, there was miles of nothing but roads heading off to only God knows where.

He had been left. Adam started to understand that he was given one of the hardest of tortures. He was left to rot. It had been a couple days since any one of the covered face men had dropped off anything that may resemble, in the slightest way, something edible. *I am left.*

One the third day of his solitude, a caped figure loomed over him. For a moment Adam thought it was the end of his life. But there were no flashbacks, no memories that came to him, he froze.

'Lost one, found two.' It was a female voice. Soft, yet brisk. She passed him a canteen of water. The water was his elixir of life, the only entity that kept him alive. Tom had never let him down. In fact Tom was the only reason why he was still alive. *How did he find me? That bastard, he was supposed to stay with her.* Every day since Adam had left her side he envied Tom. Never before had he felt such a jealous streak, but he knew that Tom would take care of her.

'Two we use, one we throw away.' The mysterious woman took off her hood as she heard Adam say this. And that was that.

He had only been riding for five minutes before she spoke. 'We are heading to the Cairo Airport.' She spoke in a thick accent, but Adam had been in the country long enough to understand. He didn't question her either, she let him drive, that was good enough. It took them two hours in an unknown direction, the sun was too high in the sky as it was mid-afternoon. Two hours to arrive to a small town where a black vehicle was waiting for them.

The woman took off with her bike before Adam could even step into the car. He half expected that Tom or one of his men was going to be waiting inside, but there was no one he recognized.

'How long will we be?' There was no answer.

Adam started to feel panicked, but kept calm nonetheless. Surely the guards at the prison he was held in would have found out he was gone by now. But could they follow? They wouldn't make a big deal, would they? If the government found out about the terrorists, it would not be Adam in a mess, it would be them. Truth be told, Adam could have been considered in the same league as those terrorists that had captured him. He had done his job successfully except for being interjected by an unexpected group and thrown into a dog cage. If they had known that he possessed over 30 million dollars in his keep, he wouldn't have been just thrown and discarded. This visit to the prison of his was the easiest he had encountered, he was not beaten or tortured. He was well fed, except until the end. They must have found no use for him. In fact they never even let him know why he was placed there in the first place. But that was beyond the matter, he was out and that was behind him. Now he had a new situation to deal with.

Adam sat, unanswered, by a group of people he didn't know. He could only see the driver through the rear view mirror, and with that he could only see his eyes. Eyes that concentrated heavily on the road in front of him. Beside him a thin, attractive, dark skinned woman dressed in a suit looked past him and out of the window. And facing him was a huge man in a light suit staring intently at him. As the time passed, there was still only silence from the other three in the car, making it only more awkward for Adam.

'Okay, does anyone know where we are going?' He tried not to express it, but he could not hide the fact that he was annoyed. There was still no answer; no one even flinched.

Adam spent over two hours in this vehicle of silence, wondering the whole time if he actually existed or had already become a spirit. His thoughts consumed him, continuing, sporadically, to desert him. He wanted to jump out of the car, but that led to nothing but more problems. He would be jumping out into an abyss of desert. Death by exhaustion or dehydration, there lay Adam Salins. If he stayed in the car, in the very least he would probably die quickly, hopefully.

Slowly at first, it was nothing but imagination becoming a growing reality. The city known as Cairo appeared. At first, nothing larger than a dust particle playing tricks on the eye. At the outskirts of the city, they finally stopped. The International Airport, the drop off point.

He looked intently out the window, searching in the crowd for one of his men. There he stood, tall and casual, spotless and untouched, hopefully. A small bug grew in his brain as he thought of Tom being alone with his Jen.

As Adam made his way closer to Tom, he noticed the huge smile on his face. Adam knew that everything was going to be just dandy, but at the same time wanted to slap that smile off his face. Breathe, release, relief, a breath.

'Tom, should have known that of all my men, it would be you.'

A long pause. 'Yes, you should have.'

'How did you find me?' Almost a whisper in Toms ear.

'I'm allowed secrets, it's why you need me. Here... these are fresh clothes, you leave in an hour, so I suggest you hurry. Your ticket.' Tom passed Adam a small bag and his ticket.

'Canada?' Adam looked back at Tom.

'You have a lot of explaining to do.'

'Jen?'

Tom thought Adam could forget, but that was just hope making a fool once again.

'Don't hurt her, whatever you do.' That sounded like a threat, and it was meant to.

Adam stood there curiously. *What the hell happened to his friend? What happened together?*

'I got my share?' Tom, quick to the point, brief and no shaking voice, soft and hard.

'You did, 15 US.' Adam started toward the inside of the airport, expecting his friend to follow.

'Adam?'

Turn. 'Yes?'

'She says she misses you.'

Adam retraced his steps back to his lead footed friend. 'Where are you going?'

'London.'

'Come to Canada with me.'

'This is something you gotta suffer alone.' *Walk away.*

'Well at least have a beer with me.'

'My plane is boarding now.' Tom couldn't even turn around. 'Call me when you are with her.'

'Okay.' Adam spoke softly, out of reach to Tom. Confused and found all in the same moment. Tom had fallen in love with Jen, there was no way for him to hide it. But Adam knew that nothing had happened, he would never question his friend. Adam wasn't the better man, and he knew it, he would have not done the same if roles had been reversed.

As Tom walked away, he knew what he had given up, and he couldn't figure out why. But he did not turn back, he kept going. He continued to move on like he always did. And he stayed away, believing he would be able to move on. However, that 15 million was not worth to price he had to pay, it suddenly weighed very heavily on him. Nothing would ever be worth it again.

Baby Boy

Chapter Seven

'Padre.' The boy, Marcello, laughed as he crawled over to Angelo. The little boy's arms reached out toward the person he thought was his father. 'Pad.' Angelo smiled and swiftly secured the boy into his strong arms. He became used to the idea of being called 'father' and couldn't help but treat Marcello like his own, after all he was there when Marcello came into the world, even when his mother wasn't. And I took over the role as Marcello's mother. We were this made up family for the boy, I never wanted to tell him that I was not his mom, and Angelo was not his father. This he did not need to know.

'Kate?' Angelo looked over at me, this always made my heart beat faster. I wished he'd ask me. I wished he would open his arms and hold me. And when he did, I would want it to be me, and only me that he was thinking of. I couldn't even imagine him thinking of anyone else, but I knew that it just wasn't possible. I could wait, because eventually I knew that he could love me, even if it was different. How long it would take, I did not know, but I certainly had time.

'Yes?'

'I've started painting again.'

Part of me sighed in sadness, but I knew that wasn't important at the moment. He had stopped painting for a long time after Jen had left. He had abandoned the place he was putting together, the place he wanted her, and left everything locked up.

'Angelo, that's amazing.' I couldn't think of anything better to say. I thought of Jen, if she was in my shoes she would know what to say. She had a way with words, but she would never be in my shoes. For someone so young she was graced with a gift, her soul rang deep and old. The calm safety in her voice even sounded better than anything I could say. Softer and beautiful, no competition.

Angelo stared at me holding the laughing child. 'I know, I think it is finally time. I had many offers on a few of my paintings. People willing to pay good money.'

'I am happy for you.' Did I sound real?

'You seem to be the only one.'

'What do you mean?' I felt that I already knew what he was going to say. His family aside from Caprice had been staying clear of him. Never supporting him when he needed it the most. I felt that we also both knew the reason. Some sort of guilt weighed heavily on their heads, but Angelo never came to assumptions. His sisters could hardly look at Angelo, they could hardly even look at me. Distance grew. But Angelo still supported them. Marcello stayed completely out of their lives. We both knew, but we left it unsaid.

It had been over a year since Jen had first come to stay with all of us. It took him long enough to begin painting again, but maybe this was a sign that he was moving on and getting over her. But that was a mistake, Angelo had only ever painted with a positive emotion, he now learned that it wasn't actually necessary. He finally could see.

'Hi.'

'Hello.' Adam stood in silence. Both of them couldn't find their first words. Adam stood in awe. Jen saw the good in him. She looks different awake. Although there was life in her at the hospital, as she stood in front of him, she was vibrant and full. He was lost in her.

The silence was broken by her laughter, it was an odd but a comfortable feeling as Jen wrapped her arms around him.

'It has been a while.' she whispered, with her mouth close to his ear sending shivers down his spine. He took in her scent, her touch, surprised by her embrace, he hugged her back.

'It has been.' He softly kissed her neck. 'I am so sorry it took me this long.'

'There's no need. Come, let's go.' She took his hand in hers. 'My dad is right over there, waiting.'

Adam sat, just as Tom had, all the way back to Jen's house. He, too, had never been to Canada before, this was a new start for him, unsure of every step, but wanting to move forward.

'Where's Tom?' Jen asked, expecting to see the both of them.

'He went to London.'

Jen hid her disappointment well, she knew that it was the best this way. It was time to learn to love Adam again. She had to. If they were to get married, there was no other choice. The weight. She needed to learn all about him again, something that scared her, something she looked forward to. Never stop discovering, never.

All the way home they sat in silence. Jen wanted to say something, but couldn't decide where to begin. And Adam sat there unsure of his next move, unsure of what she knew. He was, by default, engaged to this young woman who he knew nothing about, even though he was supposed too.

One step. Move. Both of their lives were about to change, both tried to prepare themselves, but there seemed no way.

It took them until they were in Jen's small room, away from her father, tightly packed in, before they spoke sincerely to one another.

'I don't know where to begin.' Jen sat nervously at the end of her bed, afraid to disappoint him.

'I know how you feel.'

Silence. Silence. Ticking of a clock, fading of light, passing of life. Silence.

'I just wish that I could remember us.'

No tears, please no tears.

'You will. You might.' Adam sat awkwardly beside her. Once he used to be good with women, once, but now there seemed nothing he could do.

'You actually think so?' There was doubt in her voice.

'What I mean is…' what do I mean? Shit. 'What I mean is… what we had, we'll have again. If it happened before , it can happen again, right?' Don't sound so unsure.

Jen wanted to reply, she couldn't have said it better. Just trust what we have.

'Look, why don't we start over again? I am willing to go through it all over again, right from the beginning. I will act like I have never met you before. You are worth it. Don't feel stressed out about anything. If you want this… we can go back to the beginning, proper and with time, we can figure each other out again.'

She sat still for along time. The silence became deafening. It caused a weird sensation, almost as though he were high.

'I think that we could make that work.' she whispered.

'It really can.' He tried to sound enthusiastic, as though it could be real.

Lost in translation between living and life. A brand new start. In the pit of her stomach something didn't feel right, but she kissed him anyway.

And so, thus began the life they were to have with each other. Questions were asked, some left unanswered. Moments of pain and of joy. Moments near death and moments that were beyond the restrictions of life. As time passed, Jen was none the wiser of certain unspoken truths. She trusted. In some ways, she trusted too much. Her suspicions ran light, if she was going to try to be happy, she had to believe whatever Adam told her. After all, why would he lie? He found it easier than he thought it would be. Easy to get lost in her, and to want to see her happy. It was the only way that he could justify to himself that it was his right to make her happy, no matter what the cost.

This relationship was no longer made up, they could feel each other, and believe that there was something that existed. They harbored secrets and feelings that would never be shared between the two of them. Their relationship was different, but it could work. Blinded by the love they thought ran deep and real. Based on lies there have been so many infamous relationships that have only turned to ashes. Based on lies their relationship could succeed.

In the heat of springs and summers and the depth of falls and winters, they both wanted to make this work. At what cost? They both wouldn't know until the time came, and it had yet to arrive.

Tears and blood, a vow and a promise. A curse, and the will to move on became only too reality. But they were happy. Happy in each others arms, happy in all its sense. Happiness as an illusion, nothing more. Life at its finest.

Self discovery: it was something I wanted. Already past thirty and my life still full of holes and no answers. Time is eating away, and I watch the boy grow. He doesn't know yet. He plays with no questions and never asking. Baby boy, what day is it? Baby boy... are you sleeping? Crying for his pillow, crying for comfort. Baby boy, forget where you come from, remember who you are. Baby boy, stay with me, you are mine, and I am yours. Baby boy, sleep now... its time to go to bed, baby boy... I love you, forget those moments, but remember me. Because... I love you. Baby boy?

Filed Memories

Chapter Eight

Little tiny souls everywhere. Running, playing, bouncing off each other. Only these souls are larger than I could possibly imagine. Their auras bursting with acceptance, trust and innocence. When did we loose that innocence? When did I? We are not even aware of the loss until we look down at the simple yet complete life of a child. It is so complex for us to be that simple. Simple in the terms of divine and natural.

All the children played, I couldn't even count they were moving too fast. Some played in groups and others alone, in corners, with their toys. I wondered what went through their minds. Play school was a good way to get Marcello into hanging out with other kids his own age. I wanted to be with him all day, but he needed someone else besides me. Even though he was just past three both Angelo and I thought that it was important to give him this time. And I saw that he loved it. It was him that led the group of children on adventures; if he could have a cape and a plastic sword at his side, he would. He entertained the whole group as I waited to pick him up. Even the children that sat alone looked up. Maybe they wished that they could be him, but maybe not.

One toy he would never let go of was his plane. I bought it once for him at a stand in the market, he spotted it out all the way across the place, and was determined to have it. It took me a while to figure out what he wanted, but as soon as he could reach, he grabbed it and wouldn't let it go. I had no choice but to buy it, otherwise I would have had to steal it, and I was not in the mood to run.

'He will be a captain one day.'

With a jump I turned to look beside me. I had not heard Angelo sneaking up on me.

'I didn't know that you were coming to pick him up today.'

'I did not know that I was. But I had time.'

He looked excited as he watched Marcello playing with the other children. I watched him now, and wondered if he ever took a moment to watch me. I looked at the other parents around the room watching their children, everyone must have felt the same as us.

It had been over three years since Jen had left. I wondered if she would ever look like these other parents at her child again. Marcello wouldn't even know, he wouldn't remember, it was just not possible. By Marcello she was forgotten, but by us she could never be. Angelo had given up some sort of effort, but he still looked intently everywhere he went. Once he said to me, 'I feel as though I will see her serving at a little café, and one day I would sit down at the table and she would ask me what I would like, but I would see that it was her, and she would see that it was me, and I would know that she never meant to leave, but it was something that couldn't be helped Stupid thought, isn't it?'

I wanted to slap him, shake him and tell him that there was no point, but I didn't. What kind of dream land did he live in? How could she never have meant to leave? There was no excuse, the only excuse that we would except would be that she had mysteriously died or been killed, and was never accounted for. Stupid thought? Yes Angelo, I think that it is. But I didn't want to think about that, not right then, not in this perfect moment. I came back to the playschool and continued happily waiting.

'I want to take you out tonight.'

What? He didn't just say that, did he?

'Do you have something nice to wear? I have a lot I want to tell you.'

'Yes?'

'Si? We will drop Marcello off with Caprice, she can take care of him for the evening. This evening it will only be us two.' He smiled, and he almost melted me. I have been waiting for this.

As we left the play school with little Marcello in our arms, I smiled. My whole body smiled. Maybe this was it. I walked away with my head held high and giggled.

Three Years Later

'Jen, I really think that you should come with me tonight.' Connie spoke in her excessively energized manner, as she always did. It was something that Jen loved about her, never once did it annoy her, the energy that Connie created only soaked into Jen and shared it with her. And at this point in her life, it seemed like all she needed was energy. Never before had she felt so tired and so consumed.

' I will, I think… I have to see what Adam is up to.' Always a good excuse.

'Who cares, really, this Art Show will be amazing. Bring Adam if you have to. Besides, you know how long Mr. Jenks has worked on getting this artist to come out here? He even flew him out.'

Jen knew she couldn't get out of this one. No excuses. She really liked Mr. Jenks, he was a great professor, and he really had a passion for the arts, but something inside her hesitated: this Art Show she knew nothing about. Normally, she did her research, checked out the works, got to know about the artists professional history, but this time she didn't even know the artist's name. Was it some big secret, or had she been too focused in that month to care? She didn't know what bothered her more, whether or not the artist was from Italy, a place that still haunted her, or the fact that her art presentation was not finished and due first thing in the morning.

'What time is it again?' Knowing fully well the time.

'9:00pm.'

'Okay.'

'What? I didn't hear you' Connie spoke quite sarcastically.

Jen couldn't help but release a smile and shake her head. 'Alright. Yes I'll go.'

'Yes… see I knew I would be able to sway you into coming.' She laughed.

'Sounds good.' Jen slightly shouted as they separated on their usual path. 'See you soon.'

'Thanks Jen.' with a slight wave.

As Jen walked further down the path she stopped and shouted. ' But

I have nothing to wear!' The only response that came back to her was that of a random couple giggling and a lonely bird squawk. No evidence of Connie ever hearing. The walk back to Jen's house from the University campus was not a far one. Adam and Jen had decided, upon her acceptance into the program, that it would be a good idea to be close to school. And in the autumn, it was beautiful.

Golden leaves, crisp air, and warm patio nights. Jen couldn't figure out when autumn had become her favorite season, but somewhere at the back of her mind she wished it would stay like that forever. Nothing more beautiful, nothing more peaceful- peace was what she needed. The skies brought that to her, the way the wind blew against her skin, making her aware of herself. Her physical self, strong and young and beautiful, but more importantly it brought her back to her mental self. Her mental self, something that she was only hanging onto by a thread, something that if ever so delicately touched would snap and drop like a dead apple falling from a tree, left rotten and dirty until it decomposed into something else. This was her number one wish. She loved Adam, she loved the Art program that she was in, and she seemed to love life, but nothing would let her forget of what her mind let go of. Never leaving a clue of where to turn to, and what to bring back. She knew that somewhere in the massive maze that was her mind it was there, all of it, all these memories. But maybe, before she decided to sleep she had chosen to lock it, place it away and never remember. Could something have been that bad? Every day, when thinking of nothing else, she was forced to make up illusions and memories that her mind no longer possessed. Jen was able to convince herself that these fake facts were reality, and started to actually believe them. The mind became a powerful tool that only seemed to work against her. It was proven to her that before she could get better, she would have to get worse. And over the years that passed, she had her ups and downs.

However, the autumn, like many other things, took its time to come back and, like many things, it went away. The wind became cold and her memories were left frozen in time, forgotten, yet there. Jen always thought that if she could chip hard enough there would be that moment of discovery. Discovery: something needed in her life, to feel complete and whole again, she would need to discover. But until then, until that moment came she would have to figure out ways to get there, while telling everyone else that she was as happy as could be, and hiding her pain to herself. Until then she would hold her head up high.

Each step on the way home was a memory being created. Something that she could remember, but at night before she would go to sleep she would shed a tear in fear that she would wake up two years later and this time she would have no one.

Tonight she would go home, work on her project, change into her most elegant outfit and walk into the Art Show of some Italian artist. She would laugh and smile and drink, but at night she would still go to bed with a tear. *When will the tears stop? Lord ,can you hear me? What do I have to do to return to peace?*

Child Of?

Chapter Nine

I miss Australia. When I first left it was to find something new. Italy was not my first choice, but it was my first opportunity. When I left I thought I would never want to go back home. I wasn't running away, I was wanting something different. I felt stuck on this continent in the middle of no where. But now more than anything I miss it. It has been years, and all the sudden one day I wake up with this desire to return home. I always kept in contact with my family, now more then ever. I thought about how they must miss me. I became proud of myself, at least they knew where I was, not lost in the abyss like others, one in particular. I felt obligated in a natural way to keep in touch with the people that I knew, never leaving behind.

I sent my family pictures, the little boy from when he was a baby, they knew everything. 'Kate, be careful.' was all my mother would ever say, most the time it would make me angry, but I couldn't keep pretending: Marcello was not my child.

Angelo was going to take Marcello with him everywhere, and what was I supposed to do, follow? It was now in my life where it was my decision to stay or go. I needed to live my life, not step the shadows of another. I wanted to be her, but I never could be. Was it time for me to go home and start my own life, find my own man? Someone that would love me as much as Angelo loved Jen? Create my own Baby Boy? I couldn't help but believe Marcello was mine, he was my Baby Boy, and no one would take that away from me. An odd obsession became my reality.

She arrived in style, like she always did. A vision, a form, herself as Art. Heads turned, bodies tensed and whispering stopped, as always. A black satin dress, long slim and elegant, curved with her body. To top that off a delicate colored scarf. All typical, but out of the black dressed crowd, she stood out. Style like everyone else. In one hand a small designer purse and in the other: Adam.

It didn't take much convincing for her to talk Adam into coming - a simple question and a quick answer: 'yes.' He was interested in Art, seemed to know more about it than anyone she had ever met, the value more than anything else. She never saw him doodle or draw or paint or do anything creative, but he had the eye.

'Thanks for coming.' She squeezed his hand tighter, and he kissed her on the cheek.

'Of course Babe.'

'We don't have to stay long… you know, make some sort of appearance a quick glance.'

'Don't worry. I'm here as long as you want me.' He smiled.

You are too good to me.

The doors opened and the air seemed hard to breathe as they pushed their way into a group of people. The place was crammed, no room for escape, people in every direction.

'I'm never going to find Connie in this mess.' *Mood faltering... shit.* 'Look, I'm going to call her on my cell in the washroom, I might be actually be able to hear something in there. I'll be right back, do whatever.' A quick kiss and she was in search for the washroom before he could even respond.

'Alright.' He smiled. Adam could tell that Jen was about to snap, too many people for her taste. The easiest idea he could proceed with was right back outside for a quick exit with a fresh air smoke.

Outside was just as busy, it took a few minutes to break from the crowd, into his own space. Adam took the opportunity and leaned against the brick wall before lighting up his cigarette. He took a deep breathe, Jen was starting to begin her uncontrollable emotions again. When this happened, Adam could do nothing but watch. She couldn't accept help from him, no matter how hard she tried. She also tried to hide it, but life wouldn't let it. Adam would work through it, he would do anything, including giving her the space she needed.

'Can I borrow a light?' A man who seemed to be walking by stopped and leaned up against the wall beside him.

'No problem.' Adam handed his lighter to the stranger. 'You Italian?'

'Si.'

Adam smiled; 'where you from?'

'Veniza.'

'Beautiful.'

'You have been?'

'Yes, a few years ago, for business.'

'You cannot go to Veniza on business, it is for the business of life and love, not work.'

Adam laughed, the stranger was right but sounded rather sarcastic at the same time. Was there something Adam was missing?

'You are right about its beauty, however.'

'Why are you here now?' Adam asked after a long pause in the conversation.

'I am the artist to the Exhibit that is taking place.' He spoke passively; not proud, but sad. There was something odd about this Artist, but his paintings were worth a handful.

'Oh wow, it is an honor.' Adam held out his hand for the stranger to accept it. 'It is probably very nice to see so many people.'

'Si, but people do make me tired.' What he didn't say was with every woman, he wouldn't give up until he saw their face. He could never forget her face. 'I am always worried that someone is going to knock something down. I think I might continue for a walk.'

'Well, it was nice to meet you.'

'Very.'

'Best of luck.'

'Thank you, hope you enjoy.'

And with that, the curious artist walked slowly and nostalgically away.

'Connie, it is so crazy busy in here. All these people.' Jen looked around uncomfortably. Too many emotions from too many people, block it away.

'I know, isn't it great?' Connie's excitement and energy grew, only this time it didn't soak into Jen.

'Yes, but... there are too many people. I wonder where Adam went?' *Its time to go. Its time to go and I haven't even seen any art yet.*

'He can take care of himself, and in the meantime, let us look at this art.' Connie looped her arm in Jen's and pulled her along to the walls of brilliance.

The first painting they stopped at was somewhat familiar. Familiar in the sense, *I am home.* Familiar in the sense of comfort.

'Wow, look at this painting.' Connie stood close, almost too close. She inspected the craftsmanship, every line, every color, its technical being. And Jen just stood, dropping anything she knew of technical knowledge in a painting, leaving the boundaries of the Art Exhibit.

'I know this painting.' She spoke more or less to herself. 'I know this painting.' This time Connie could hear Jen and was broken away from the painting.

'You know this painting? From where?'

'I've seen it before. I mean in physical existence. This painting has played over and over in my dreams.'

'Something like it you mean?'

'No this is it, paint line for paint line.'

'Good Artist then, huh?' Connie wasn't sure she could believe her.

'Yes, but I don't know what that has to do with this. It is like he pulled this image from my mind to the outside. I must have painted this in my past life.'

'Okay, hun, you are starting to freak me out. Do you want to move on?'

'No, sorry Connie, I need to stay here and watch this painting for a little longer.'

With that, Connie moved on, and Jen couldn't blink.

'This artist is confused. Confused in a way of loneliness. Confused in a way of hope. In this particular painting, the subject or the underlining artist has just lost something. Something that had the ability to cast off one shot of a thought. This shot then becomes trapped into this painting. The detail painted on the hand shows the ability of one person's capability. The shades of greens and browns in the background not only promote a life style of health and beauty, but a distant comfort that is not yet in grasp because it is not clear but blurry. The lines on the hand show paths that the subject, or the artist, has the ability to take, and hasn't yet chosen. One path looks clear and long while the other has many turns and bends. Moreover, the viewer knows before the artist does which path must be chosen.' What was going on? There was no explanation, but something reminded her of these words. There was no reason for it.

The place was starting to get busier before Jen was pushed and forced to move on. Nothing made sense to her. She couldn't figure it out. How did this artist paint her dreams? Had they met before? She had to move on.

This Art Show was also marked for the re-opening of the building. It sat on the edge of the University Campus, abandoned for too long. It was a historical building to the city and for so long it had been left to melt away only in the memories of its surroundings. When Mr. Jenks approached the University, they agreed that it would be a good idea to start using the building again. Its closed doors opened, and it filled with people, some curious about what the inside looked like, others curious about the artist. It was a well hidden secret, both the Artist and the building, a perfect event.

'Hey, Mr. Jenks.' Jen saw him wandering nervously around the small bar. She needed to put that painting away. Lock it in her mind and burn it later. At the moment Mr. Jenks was free, which was probably the first time all night. She needed to show him that she had made at least some sort of effort to come.

'Hello, Jennifer, how's it going?' The man had style, he didn't look like he was an arts professor, he looked more like a high end business man, with a designer suit. Every student of his definitely had a thing for him, female or male it didn't seem to matter, bringing everyone back to their Junior High days.

'Oh, good. I can't believe the turn out, this is amazing.' *It really is. Even if I can't breathe.*

'It is, isn't it.'

The one attribute Mr. Jenks had over everyone else was his ability to pay full attention and devotion to the moment. Although a million thoughts must have crossed his mind, he paid all his attention to Jen, never looking past her.

'Jennifer, did you get a chance to meet the Artist?'

'No. I'm not familiar with what he looks like.'

'You really should, his work reminds me of yours. I have spent a lot of time talking with him these last few days, you would get along with him well.'

'Thanks, Mr. Jenks.'

'Don't thank me. Look, Jennifer don't let this get around but I am working on a grant with the University right now… it might not follow through, but I have a really good feeling about this. How would you like to study under this Artist for three months?'

'What? Really?' *Surprise. Just breathe.* 'I am really honored, that would be… more than amazing.'

'Great, I am glad to hear that. We will talk tomorrow. Oh by the way, I am really looking forward to the presentation tomorrow. Mr. Moretti might actually have the time to check it out.'

Only a 'thanks' came out of her voice as Mr. Jenks walked away. 'Shit. I need to get that done.'

The next painting stunned Jen even more. This painting actually had a title unlike the first one, 'Our Mysterious One.' It was a little boy, he sat on stone path, his legs bent in an odd position backwards. His hand raised high, almost lost in the bright ball of the sun, but it was quite clear that he held a toy plane. A smile covered his face as he looked up past the point of the painting. Only two hands could be seen reaching for him, two mysterious arms. Jen couldn't see straight, her tears covered her eyes, tears that could not be wiped away, they were meant to be there. She couldn't tell why she was crying, unlike the other painting she had never seen this image before. However there was something beyond reality that spoke to her, unlike any other painting she had ever looked into. Who is this painter? She looked around as though she was being watched. People everywhere, she couldn't even see over any of their heads, did they even care about the art? The possessive nature she felt for this painting was overwhelming. She wanted to reach for it, take it off the wall and walk out the door. All her will power held her back. Never had she had the urge to possess something so much until this moment in her life. Without knowing why, it scared her, and threw her off guard.

Each painting came and went. They were beautiful, creative and full, but they didn't catch her the way that child did. As she moved from painting to painting, the boy kept staring at her, every time she closed her eyes, he was there. Never did he become real, never did she feel him reaching for her, but that was all she longed for. The child… this child… his eyes haunting. Eyes that I recognize only in my sleep. Beautiful eyes, inside them innocence and something that was so full of content, it would make anyone forget there was such thing as sadness.

'Jen, you have to see this painting.' Connie gladly interrupted the maze of her mind.

'Sorry, what?' She returned to reality.

'Jen… you have to see this painting.' Connie started pulling Jen to another room. ' I have to warn you,' Connie spoke over the crowd as they pushed their way through, '…something is not right about it. If you found the other one frightening this one… well, Jen, I honestly don't know what to say.'

Jen thought that Connie might have been overreacting like she always did, but those last two paintings still haunted her, and made her obsessive.

As they entered the other room, Jen noticed that it was only one painting, but it was not placed high enough for her to see. As Jen made it close to the painting… her heart started to beat faster, people's voices dissipated into music. It was not until she was close enough almost to touch it before she could see clearly and focus on what was in front of her. It was not until than that she realized.

Sudden tears welled up in her eyes, shaking, breathing… her body closing down, trying to stop. All these paintings were too much for her to handle, a missing part of her life. And finally this one? The grand finale? There was something wrong. I am dying. *I am going to go back into that coma, and I am going to die.* It felt all too real.

'Jen… Jen?' She couldn't hear Connie, but the sound of some sort of lute, playing Romance de Amour in the distance of echoes.

'Excuse me, excuse me… miss? Jen could hear an elderly lady aside from the music, and didn't know why. ' I must ask…' the smiling lady couldn't tell there was anything wrong, 'how was it posing for this painting?' No answer. 'It is an honor to know that you are just as beautiful as what this painting shows. You truly are a Goddess. Jen lost consciousness just in time for Adam to catch her.

What was with all the commotion? Angelo thought as he walked back into his Art Exhibit. *Don't panic.* The first thought that ran through his mind was that something had happened to one of his paintings, but as soon as he heard the whisperings around the room he knew that everything was okay, and he sighed a breath of relief. 'What happened to her?' 'Do you think that she'll be alright?'

Angelo went straight for the bar; he needed to be out of the way of whatever was happening. As he moved closer to the bar, he noticed that the man he had met outside was holding a woman in his arms - she seemed lifeless. Her face covered by her hair, but her legs and arms were noticeably white, almost greenish. The man holding her looked concerned and focused.

At a time like this, Angelo couldn't help but see the detailed beauty around him. The focus on everyone's face as the man with the lifeless woman walked quickly by. Everyone faded into the background. Smudged pastel colors, darker at first then lighter as the eye reached the centre. The moment was perfect. Only one thing distracted Angelo from the vision's perfection. If only Angelo could move the hair from the woman's face. He would have to imagine it, her red ruby lips partly opened. Her eyes would be closed, but her lashes long and sexy, just like the curve of her black dress that flowed over her perfect body. The man holding her... concentration and love openly seen across his face. His arms strong and muscular, clutching her tight to his chest.

The moment seemed to go slowly. The lack of a heartbeat that made everything whole... yet the continuing of life lingered in the air, and like everything else these moments end.

'Sorry about all this commotion.' Mr. Jenks stood beside Angelo. Where did he come from? How much time had actually passed? Beside Mr. Jenks was a young woman, worry covered her face, something she did not even try to hide.

'No need to apologize.' Angelo took a drink of fine Italian wine from the bar, the kind that came out of a box. 'She is your friend, Si?'

'Yes...' Connie spoke softly, unusual for herself. 'Jen will be fine. She... hasn't been feeling well for the last couple of days. I forced her out here... I feel so...'

'Sorry... what did you say her name is?'

'Jen.'

'She was the student that I was talking to you about.' Mr. Jenks cut in.

'Oh... right.' It had been along time since Angelo had heard that name. He knew that in Canada that name wasn't uncommon. He rationalized and knew how unlikely that it was the young woman he once knew beyond reality. Once, long ago, he knew a Jen, Jennifer, but now there was another. Hope had certainly never abandoned him, but that only left him hanging onto something that no longer existed.

'You would be very interested in her work. Hopefully she will still be able to do her presentation tomorrow.'

'Mr. Jenks, I'm not sure, she might need some rest.' Connie cut in, no longer timid with her voice but strong and hyper, hitting Angelo's ear drum in a foul way.

'Yes, you are probably right.' Mr Jenks took his time turning hesitantly to Mr. Moretti and spoke slowly. 'I would still like you to come in tomorrow and take and look at her portfolio, it is brilliant.'

'Of course.'

'Thank you, I really look forward to this exchange.'

The two men stood there quite curiously to Connie. Her mind wondered as they continued talking. *Was that really a picture of Jen? Where did he find her? What is this inspiration?* Connie wanted to interrupt the two men's conversation, but decided against it. Something wasn't right, something was missing. The picture could very easily be someone else. Someone that looked like her, but not her, could it be? A small streak of jealousy quickly passed through her. How beautiful she really is! Connie herself, was a beautiful young lady, but like over ninety percent of the female population in North America, it was impossible to feel comfortable with the way that she looked. Jen was also different from the ideal females posing on the front page of magazines, Connie thought, but there is something about her. Her classic look, her haunting eyes, and her aura took over an entire class without her even realizing it. When it is told or heard about people that HAVE IT, she is the one being talked about.

'Connie, can I get you a drink?' The Artist man said, bringing her back to reality.

Quite casually and not thinking about much else she answered; 'yes.'

'What can I get for you?' His accent so exotic, his voice luxurious. Connie couldn't help but start a childhood crush.

'Screwdriver.'

'I am sorry?'

'Oh, shit, sorry, vodka and orange juice would be lovely. Thank you.' Angelo tried not to laugh as he watched the young lady try and compose herself.

It only took a moment to gain the bartender's attention, and he was back.

'Here you are, madam.'

'Thank you. How did you know my name?' *When did I tell him my name?*

'Mr. Jenks said it just now in passing conversation.' Connie subtly looked around as he spoke, *when did Mr. Jenks leave?*

'I am Angelo Moretti.'

'Yes, I know. Beautiful work, I can't get over it.' *And neither can Jen.*

'Grazie, I am honored to be here.'

There was a sudden rush of people to the bar, which forced Connie and Angelo to move into a tight corner. It was hard to believe but it seemed as though even more people had arrived. There must be some sort of fire code issue.

'So Mr. Moretti...'

'Please just call me Angelo.'

'Alright. Angelo, how long are you here for?'

'I leave tomorrow night.'

'Really, so soon?' Connie tried hard not to sound disappointed. 'Guess you don't want to leave your wife for too long.' Nosey.

'I am not married.'

'A man of your looks? That is hard to believe.'

'Thank you.' He saw what she was trying to do. 'My fiancée decided to stay home and look after my son.'

'Oh.' Damn he's taken. 'Lucky woman.'

And with that Connie thanked him for the drink and bid him farewell. It was time to go and see if her friend was okay.

***

There is a lost beauty that exists in one that suffers with grace. Whether it be a physical or mental suffering, and whether that brings that person to an end or heightens their capability, there lies a lost beauty. Left alone in her mind, nothing could stop the random thoughts that would eventually drive a person to insanity. These events that happen in a person's life that can never be undone, and pushes them into a stance. In her, this needed to stop.

There is a story that everyone knows, but this story has never been told or explained. The only way this story can be explored is through a feeling. It is not a myth or a legend, but a story. And that is where Jen found herself when she fell out of consciousness.

She stood there, unsure of where she was. The images around her were faded and colorless. She walked with no shoes and there was no mistake of feeling the old cold cobblestone wet against her feet. There inevitably seemed to be only one direction, and as visually unclear as that direction was, it never felt more clear in her mind the way she was supposed to go.

In front of her a figure, an unknown shape moving slightly as if the figure was breathing. The closer she got to this figure, the more details and colors came around her. It was a boy... it was that boy. The boy who looked at her in the painting. He sat in the same way with the toy plane in his one hand, smiling up at the person who was left unknown in the painting. It became clear to Jen who that unknown person was: it was her. The artist knew it too, even if they had never met before, there could be no other way.

And now in her story she reached the boy, her arms outstretched towards him. The boy smiles, and stands to be embraced by her.

She catches him in her arms, she lifts him and holds him close. He holds on tight and warm. He smells like something familiar, something from somewhere a long time ago… tea, he smells like tea.

She can't let him go, she feels every emotion go through her veins, as though her blood has dissipated. He leans into her and places his head on her shoulder, and whispers: 'Don't worry, it's okay.' He was right, at that moment, everything was okay.

However, this is the part of the story where she wakes up, and concludes that none of what happened was real. And in the future she will continue on with her days constantly thinking about this boy and trying to forget the impossible. He is only a figment of her imagination, nothing else. Time to continue… only to wake up.

Since he had met her, life had become a hub of interesting events. He could have left her, dropped her from his mind the way he was supposed to, but he saw something else. It was his opportunity for a change. How he ever ended up in his line of work was a mystery to him, but it became an addiction; it was no longer about the money. It was an obsession that could have his life had he not met her. Jen: the definition of mystery. In the last three years of being with her not a single memory had retraced and found her. What if she woke up to find the last three years of their life missing? Or worse yet, what if she found herself remembering what was supposed to be never retraced?

Adam carried Jen outside through the oversized doors, hailed down a cab, and without questioning went straight to the hospital. There was no long wait in the emergency, she was immediately admitted and taken out of Adam's reach, where he was asked to wait.

The night had started out in an unusual way for him. Jen had been acting strangely since she had come home from school. Jen was required to go to these Art shows at least once a week, people from all over the world had come through that program, what was so different about this one? Tonight she was uneasy and nervous, the first sign something was wrong. Adam had went outside for a smoke, and when he came back and made his way through the crowd, it was just in time to catch her faint. Adam knew too well not to chance that it was the possibility of just a faint. What if she was about the lapse into another coma? He paced back and forth in the waiting room, wondering, worrying and forgetting to breathe. It was over an hour before someone came to speak with him, and hour of thoughtless thoughts. These are the kind of hours that age a person almost a lifetime, the hours that hold an eternity.

'Mr. Adam Salins?' Her voice was calm and steady. Had she been practicing in the doctor's change room, breathing steadily? Or was everything really truly alright?

'Yes?' Eagerly waiting. He turned to see a young woman, her smile instantly cooled his inflictions.

'I'm Dr. Engle. How are you doing tonight?' Adam couldn't even answer the question. 'Jennifer Sipi is in stable condition. She is sleeping, but she will be just fine, there is no need to worry.' A moment of dizzy relief, white behind his eyes. Jen had him wrapped around anything she wanted without even knowing it. He would go through anything to make sure nothing would happen to her, she was a sorcerous.

Adam couldn't speak, he could only nod and swallow back the lump in his throat.

'You will be able to see her shortly.' The Doctor turned to walk away, and quickly turned back again, 'Oh... and Mr. Salins?'

'Yes?'

'Congratulations!' This time she walked away without turning back.

What?

Silky Skin, Long Lashes

Chapter Ten

This story had not turned out the way I had expected. I thought that Angelo could never let go of her, never let go of the memory this woman left behind. He would never want to feel another woman, especially me. The way Angelo was going, he was doomed to a lonely life and a sad ending. And if that was his reality it was going to be mine. I made a decision to dedicate what I knew of myself to this man and this boy. There was nothing in my willpower to do anything else. I had made this decision no matter what my sacrifices would be. That is why when Angelo asked me to marry him I had no choice but to say, 'yes.'

I had never expected it; I wanted it, but I never thought that he would ask me. After I said 'yes' it was the first time he had ever kissed me. I had waited for that kiss, that passionate soft kiss for my entire life. But that kiss was not it. I held it in, I never asked him 'why?,' I simply said yes. I knew in some sort of way that he loved me, and I knew that we could be happy. He loved me, but he was not in love with me. Did that really matter? He held my heart even though I didn't hold his. We were comfortable together, we had a common ground, and he knew that no matter what I would always be there for him. I was there for his worst; I deserved to be there for his best, whatever that entailed.

I stared back to see the rest of Venice. That night, like I had every night since I arrived, I prayed. I prayed that Jen would never come back to take this dream away from me.

'Good morning Jen.' Doctor Engle spoke softly as she entered the room. Jen was slowly coming back to reality, but nothing was coming clear to her.

'No one told me...' She couldn't hide her worries, her ultimate fear, escaping from her voice; '...what day is it?'

'There is no need to worry, you have only been sleeping for the night. You are doing just fine for your condition.'

'Sleeping?' Only sleeping. Jen's mind searched through all her memories, trying to recall. The image of the woman laying naked was the most vivid in her mind; the painting was beautiful. In her mind she lay against the warm sheets, looking out to a place she had once been. It was a memory, but the wrong one. A man beside her, his form blurry, his hands clear and full of paint. Jen opened her eyes, she could focus on nothing. Voices, all unknown to her surrounding the air.

'Jen?'

When she woke up again there was more than the one doctor around her. *What had happened?*

'Am I okay?'

'Yes, Jen, we are trying to stabilize your blood pressure.'

Was time passing by or did everything turn into slow motion? Either way it seemed as though an eternity had gone by before anyone spoke again.

'We have much to talk about Jen. I will let you rest, and then we can go into my office.' Jen had no energy to go against anything the doctor said. She fell back to sleep, only this time her sleep was dreamless.

She couldn't recall how she found herself walking into Dr. Engles office, but Jen found herself supported in the grasp of Adam's hands.

'Good afternoon, Jen, Adam have a seat.' Her office did not seem like a doctor's office that Jen would ever imagine. Instead of that cold clinical feeling, Dr. Engle's office was washed with oak walls and leather seats. It was warm and relaxing. The lights weren't the bright fluorescence, they were soft and soothing to the eyes.

As Jen sat down, she could feel herself sink into an abyss of comfort.

'Good afternoon.'

Dr. Engle sat down behind her desk and looked back at the worried couple. Both of the were physically there, but mentally they seemed to be missing in action. In her learned reassuring voice she spoke. ' Don't look so worried, everything will be fine.' Unlike most patients they didn't relax, they continued to hold themselves in a rigid tense posture.

'First of all... congratulations.'

Jen's first instinct to the word congratulations was to feel her stomach. The word 'congratulations' and 'pregnant' seemed to go hand in hand. However along with her first instinct came another: to play dumb and act like she didn't know what was going on.

'What do you mean... congratulations?' Everything seemed to be zooming in on her, she looked over at Adam. His reaction was almost opposite of hers. His smile could not be more pronounced, his face filled with excitement. Jen didn't know that Adam had the time to let it sink in.

'Jen, don't look so upset.' Adam slightly laughed, 'You will be a great mother.'

'Mother, I'm not ready to be a mother. I'm finishing school. I'm ... not ready.' She couldn't find the words to describe the fear. The fear of facing what her mother must have gone through, the fear of doing something wrong, the fear of the unknown.

'Jen, honey, I know you will be fine, we are doing it together.' Adam took her hand. 'You and me, babe.'

This time the tears never came, no tears of happiness, no tears of sadness, they forgot to come.

'It's hard to know your exact date, but you are ending your first trimester.' Dr. Engle tried to stay calm, but Jen's reaction was confusing her.

'End of the first trimester, and I never knew, I never knew that something was growing inside of me? End of the first trimester, that is the end of three months, right?'

'Yes, it is not uncommon that you didn't know. Especially in a case like yours.'

'A case like mine, what is my case?' Her voice stayed soft, but inside it felt as though she was going to explode. Adam's kiss on her forehead didn't seem to help.

'Well to the best of our knowledge, there might be some complications.' Dr. Engle sat at the edge of her chair. 'There is information missing in your files, I need to know some of your personal information. Jen this is something you are probably all too aware of, only this time it could be more dangerous, but there are things we can prevent.'

'Why would I be aware of this? I am confused Dr. Engle.'

'Babe, its okay. Dr. Engle, can you explain?'

'I mean her Eclampsia has returned with this pregnancy. Your first child must have been a very difficult birth. But when something like this returns, it is hard for you and the child, there is higher risks of death or paralysis. I don't mean to frighten you bu...'

'What do you mean? I think you must have mistaken me. If what you are saying is true, you have the wrong person, I have never been pregnant before and I don't ever recall having Epa... whatever it's called... I'm sorry but you must be mistaken.'

'I'm sorry Ms. Sipi...here is your personal file, it has your address as of three years ago, your date of birth, the doctor you saw when you were pregnant. The last file he left on you, it says here that you were having problems with high blood pressure, your due date and next appointment are outlined here, the only thing missing was you. I'm not sure what kind of game you are playing, but it is very obvious that you have had a child and that there were probably huge complications. If you brought that child to full term or not, I am not too sure, but I need you to cooperate with me. Do you ever remember suffering from seizures or any sort of lapses?'

'Yes, but all of that has nothing to do with a child. I had no child.'

Jen took the personal records and studied them for a moment. Something was missing, the dates didn't make any sense. The last appointment with the doctor did not fit.

'See, Dr. Engle, there must have been some sort of mistake. I understand that Dr. Fitzer is my normal family doctor, and that all this information matches me, but there is no way I could have seen Dr. Fitzer that day, I was somewhere in Europe. I left to Europe after I graduated, and was there for at least five or six months. Right, Adam?'

Adam didn't say anything back, he only nodded, lost in a time he tried not to remember.

'Alright... I'm not sure how to go about this, but I personally have run you through a few tests. By the looks of it, you gave birth to a child. I am not 100% sure because it was almost four years ago, but I am not sure what else it could be.' Dr. Engle stood up, confused but determined to state her point. 'However, the real point of this is that we find out the measures we need to go through to make sure that the child inside you now will arrive into this world with the mother alive. Needless to say, the next few month are going to be challenging. You can go home, but rest for at least a couple weeks. Please come back and see me in two weeks. We need to talk about how we are going to proceed with this pregnancy. Most importantly, please relax. Here is my card if you have any questions, please feel free to use it.' Dr. Engle sat down again, letting herself breathe. 'Everything will most likely make sense.'

There was a moment of silence between the three of them, each in their individual thought of what had just happened.

'Thanks doctor, sorry for the confusion.' Both Jen and Adam left more lost than found. Their zombie like demeanor took them home into a deep slumber. Nothing was spoken about this mysterious pregnancy, although that was the only thought that consumed their minds.

***

'Tom?'

'Yes this is. Who is this?'

'Tom, I'm surprised you can't remember my voice.'

'Adam.'

'Don't sound too happy or anything.' Adam laughed.

'What are you calling for?'

This didn't sound like the Tom Adam knew. His voice was the same, but something had changed him in the last few years.

'Tom, I need to see you.'

'What for?'

'Its about Jen, she's in trouble.'

'Where do we meet?' Something in Tom's voice changed again. There was a hidden eagerness that took over, something only Adam could point out. The conversation with Tom had left Adam feeling uneasy. Adam downed a shot of whiskey and tried to clear his mind. He always wanted to ask Jen if anything had happened with her and Tom, but never got the courage. To Tom, Jen had been a part of the job, but for Adam was it was his choice. It didn't really matter that it was him that she picked. Their lives were just starting out together, and soon they would be parents, and if all went according to plan, they would soon be married.

'Can I get you another?' The bartender asked. She had been eying Adam as soon as he entered the bar. She was beautiful, but hid nothing of what she felt, there was no mystery to her. Adam guessed that she was probably in her early forties. 'Or can I bring you anything else?'

'You want to have a shot with me?'

'Couldn't hurt, I guess.' There was a little grin that spread across her face as she poured the drinks. 'Trouble in paradise?'

He was hardly in paradise.

'Just a little.'

'Look, I don't say this often, and I wish I didn't have to say this to you, but go home.'

'Well, that makes me feel wanted.' Adam couldn't help but slur his words as he shot the drink back, and stood up. 'But you are probably right, I think that I am needed right now.'

After putting on his coat and paying up he stumbled out of the bar. The walk home was long, but not long enough. His thoughts absorbed him. He kept repeating in his mind over and over the first time he met her, she was running from him, he was instructed to kill her. There was no way she could have been pregnant, was there? Even in her fear, she was beautiful. When Adam first saw her fall, he thought it was the fall alone that had put her in a coma. Now nothing was making sense. Everything, all of it was supposed to be gone, buried and forgotten. He didn't notice the small amount of rain that sprinkled onto him, he was lost in a past that was never meant to be brought up. There was no way he could tell Jen if she was pregnant or not. What happened to the child? Was it left alone abandoned, or was it dead at birth? Was he the one responsible for the separation of Jen and her child?

Tears blended in with the rain. Tears that Adam had forgotten about. He couldn't remember the last time he had cried, he couldn't remember the last time it had rained either. He looked up lost in the falling rain, feeling like he was falling with it.

It was time to go face Jen, tell her he didn't know, he didn't know the truth. He stood outside the door to their place, his hand stayed placed on the handle, ready to be turned, wishing with all his power that things could go back. Facing her was going to be the hardest part. Looking her in those beautiful eyes, the eyes that looked right into him, and tell her a lie. This was something he had never anticipated. Finally the courage came to open the door, when he saw a figure beside him.

'What's holding you back?' Tom stepped into the patio light, soaking wet like Adam. Before Adam could reply he had to gain his breath and control his heart rate.

'Tom, God I thought that you weren't coming until tomorrow.' Adam reached to him for a old friendly hand shake but Tom walked right past him.

' I came as early as I possibly could.' He stood against the door, away from the rain. 'As soon as you told me that you needed to see me, I booked my flight.'

There was a moment between the two; both knew that they had missed each other, and both knew what lied between them. Adam studied Tom, as Tom studied Adam. Tom had become what Adam was, before he had met Jen. His face more chiseled, his eyes darker, his posture more demanding. Time had been hard on him, crushing him to what he had become. When Tom looked back at Adam he saw that time had done the complete opposite for Adam. Adam had become soft, as though he lost his outer shell. He was naked. Seeing Adam like this made Tom's eyes lighter, this is when they shared that moment.

'It has been too long.' Tom unexpectedly gave Adam a grasping hug.

'It has been. I am glad to see you, old friend.' Adam hugged him back. 'Let's go inside. Jen is asleep, I don't want to wake her.'

Tom inspected the inside of their place and tried not to laugh, he even hid his smile. Never in Tom's world would he have expected Adam to be living in a place like this. It was beautiful, warm and comfortable. It was welcoming and, to say the least, artistic. Why had Adam not moved into some sort of mansion, the one he always talked about? The one with marble hallways and twenty foot tall ceilings, the one that sported a pool, a six car garage, and no clutter. Adam hated clutter.

'Nice place you got here.' Tom took off his soaking coat and Adam hung it next to the door.

' Yeah, its nice for now, we will get something else when Jen's school is finished. She likes it here.'

'It reminds me of her.' Tom got lost in that scent he could vividly remember as her, the girl he knew.

'Excuse me?'

'Oh... it looks like something she would like. Warm, comfortable... a home.' A home was still something that Tom didn't have, and the way his thoughts were going, it felt like he never would.

'Would you like something to drink, what about Merlot? I remember you always liked fine wines.' Adam already made his way to the kitchen. On the small wooden table and all the counters it looked as though there were pieces of sculptures everywhere, and newspapers covered the ground.

'Oh... shit. Jen didn't know that you were coming, she has an art project due at the end of the week, it was kind of left here, I just forgot about it.' Adam continued to pour drinks.

'Instead of stealing them you make them... more classy.' Tom laughed.

'She's very good, one day they will be worth more than anything we ever stole.'

'I can see that.'

As soon as they got comfortable in the living room Tom cut to the chase.

'Why Adam? Why did you get me to come all the way here?'

'Tom, Jen is in some sort of trouble.' Adam sat uneasy, at the edge of his seat.

'What's wrong?'

'Well she's pregnant.'

Those words made Tom swallow hard, and hoped that the deepest of his jealousy stayed hidden within him.

'Shouldn't you be jumping for joy?' Tom couldn't help but be cynical, 'you know like yeah.'

'Don't look so enthused.' Adam laughed.

'Why should I be, you don't look to happy about it either.'

'Well I am, we are... there's more to it. We were at an Art Show the other night when Jen passed out, I took her to the hospital, she was attended to right away. When we saw the doctor, we were told that Jen would have some complications like her last pregnancy.'

Tom cringed, he could not believe that he came from the other side of the country for this, he almost wanted to stand up and walk out that door but he knew that upstairs in some room lay Jen, that need to see her was overwhelming. He was too close to her, too close to leave.

'I still don't get why I am here, Adam,'

'Tom... Jen never had another child.'

'Ohhh...' Tom's mind stopped if only for a second. It stood still, and when it continued it moved fast. Something had gone terribly wrong. There was a sudden chill that went through Tom's spine as he looked at Adam. Memories of the past started coming up.

'Its probably some sort of mistake. Its easy enough to have the wrong files, did she even get a chance to look at them?'

'Yes, she did. They came from her. Files on her appointments, her due date, any complications. The only thing was... she just disappeared. She never showed up for her last appointment scheduled with her doctor. There is no record of her giving birth. No child, no birth certificate, nothing.' Adam's voice settled into a erie calmness as he drank back some wine.

'Okay, well did they even think that she might have had a miscarriage? Maybe a stillborn?' *What was it the Italian doctor said?*

'That is a possibility, although the doctor did say that she did give birth to a child, there is a possibility that anything could have happened.' It was at that point when Adam's voice started to quiver.

He never cried, or altered the look in his face, but there was a internal fight that was going on in his mind, one that only showed through his eyes and voice. Tom still knew him well enough to see that.

'Maybe, Adam, it's better that she doesn't remember what happened. Maybe she is where she is now because there was a reason in fate, she needed to forget the fact that she gave birth to a stillborn. Maybe she wouldn't have been able to live with herself, had she remembered.' Tom stopped... trying to recall anything, something from over three years ago. Knowing that what he said was only to comfort Adam, his old friend, a stranger that looked back at him now, a man full of guilt, full of something that was only his to bare.

'Tom, I want to know... when you were with her is there anything that might have indicated in any way that she had just gone through child birth? Anything that the doctor might have said or she might have gone through? Anything?'

There was something Tom recalled... but he never wanted Adam to know this, that was a different story. Tom sat in silence, staring off past Adam, as though he was watching a memory. Watching over three years ago, the angel that lay in front of him, lost to the rest of the world. Watching as her breasts started to lactate, wondering what was going on, but never telling anyone about it. The doctors mentioned something, however, there was no way he could tell Adam.

'Is this why you brought me here?' Tom tried to delay the subject, he knew that couldn't hide the truth from this man. Adam held the gift of knowing someone was lying, thats why he was so good at his job: he could read right through someone. 'You brought me here just to ask me that question?'

There was a delay in Adam's response. The time had come where Adam had to ask Tom another favor, too many favors, he just did not know what he would do if Tom said 'no.' 'No' could be such a powerful word. Adam always had a way to get Tom to say yes, but it had been over three years since he had last seen him, quite noticeably things had changed.

'No. That's not the only reason.' Adam leaned forward in his chair, cradling the glass of wine in his hand. 'I need you to do a job for me, it will be like old times.'

Tom held the laugh in his throat. 'Right, old times.'

'Tom, there is this painter. The night Jen and I went to the hospital we were at an Art Show. Jen felt reluctant to go, I know now that she must have been feeling sick. But I saw a piece that looked like a goddess, painted naked, lying there with Venice in the background. I believe he painted her there, on the Giudecca Canal looking back at Venice.

'Adam, let me get this straight... you think Jen is in a painting now?'

' Yes.'

'So this artist some how found her and painted her?' His sarcastic note hit Adam hard.

'I know it sounds ridiculous, but I'm telling you...'

Tom stood up trying not to show his anger. 'Right, Adam, what do you want... you want me to steal this worthless painting of someone who looks like your girlfriend to find out if...' Tom never finished this rampage: he turned away from Adam, trying not to show Adam his true feelings. In the moment of the pause it was disturbed by a loud gasping noise that came from upstairs. The gasping was laboured and sounded painful, both men stood up in alert.

'Jen?!' Tom was waiting to see her, but to hear her like this was something that made his stomach turn.

'Yes?' Adam ran upstairs with Tom following close behind, both unaware of their steps, trying not to panic.

'Where is she?' Nothing was heard, it was lost into the air with no answer.

It was Adam who saw her first, but his mind and body froze when he saw her. She sat fully clothed in the tub, hot water steamed the room, making it hard to see her. In the tub she sat, her legs bent up to her chest and her arms cradling them. She cried silently. Unaware of the two men in front of her, she cried. The water continued to pour out of the tub at a rapid rate. Tom only stopped for a moment to read the situation. It was Adam who was supposed to go after her, it was Adam, not Tom. However, Adam stood, frozen with no efforts to console her.

Tom made his way through the river of water pooling around the entrance and turned off the running water. 'Ow.' The water felt as though it burnt his hands, yet Jen was emerged right in it, sitting there unaffected. 'God, Adam, what are you doing?'

Tom looked over at both of them. Adam, Jen, *what was going on?* Their bodies where still there, but lost in a distant world was the rest of them. Tom reached into the water to pull out the plug trying to ignore its heat, the water almost felt as though it was boiling. With no hesitation he wrapped his arms around her and pulled her out of the tub.

'Come on Jen, it's okay.' Tom said this more to reassure his own well being. She lifted her head right towards him, but her eyes looked past him. She looked tired and helpless as though she had given up, as though there was no point, but she clung to him. She held to him like she did when Tom pulled her from the ice water. Her wet clothes steamed as they left the washroom, her skin scolding red. Tom's feelings for this woman could not be hidden as he held her. Adam stood there still lost in another world. 'You like me pulling you out of the water, don't you?' A lost joke. 'No wonder everyone can fall in love with you, I just want to take care of you.' Pause. 'Adam, get over here.' Tom yelled in his deep scruffy voice. 'What the hell is going on with you?' Tom placed her softly on the bed.

Adam came from the washroom, he looked as though he had seen a ghost.

'Hey man you okay?' What was Adam doing? *I would never abandon her when she needed me the most.*

'I'm sorry, I...' All the blood had rushed away from his face, his voice was shaky.

'Don't apologize to me, look at her - she needs you.'

They both looked over at Jen, she lay on her side curled up as though she were a child.

'Tom, I didn't know what I have done.'

'Are you trying to get me to tell you that you did nothing wrong?' Tom stood between both Jen and Adam. 'Adam, you took her life away.'

Adam walked slowly up to him. There they stood, side by side staring down at her. 'I did, didn't I.' Adam knelt down beside her, and wiped the small water droplets off her face. She had fallen asleep, her clothes soaking the bed. The absent sadness dissolved now into a peaceful sleep. Her wet hair sculpted down the side of her face down her neck and over her shoulder. Tom watched as Adam placed a kiss on her brow, wanting to kill that man, but knowing he never could.

'Yes, but you gave her another one.' Tom turned away. He couldn't look at her any more. In the three years since he had seen her, she had become even more beautiful, if that was actually possible. She was a woman, the curves in her body the features in her face and the energy that hovered over her. Silky skin, long eye lashes and full lips, life.

'Adam, where is my room?' It been a long day.

'Just across from this one.'

'Thanks.' Pause. 'Adam, I'll do what you ask.' Tom never turned around to look at Adam. Instead, he stared at the small details in the wood of the cedar molding. Once again, Tom walked away.

Going to Sleep

Chapter Eleven

'Kate.' I looked over at the little boy, who just said my name. He stood there looking up at me, wide eyed and full of excitement. I wish that he would call me 'mom' but he never did, it felt like it would never happen. Yet he called Angelo his father, no one ever told him, or corrected him, it just stayed that way.

'Yes, Marcello?' We started walking down the market in Burano. He liked looking at the brightly painted fishing homes, and the island was the place where his favorite little park sat. Today, as we walked to the park, I noticed the clouds make their way overhead, and I hoped that we wouldn't be stuck in the rain.

'What does she look like?' Marcello innocently asked. He could speak English just as well as he could speak Italian. I always had a little laugh when he would mix both the languages together. I was thrown off guard by the question, it had been along time since Marcello had even spoken of her.

'What does who look like?'

'My mom.' Marcello was almost four, he wasn't old enough to ask these questions and I wasn't ready to tell him.

I knelt down in front of him and looked him straight in the eye. I held both of his hands, and squeezed. Nothing could take me from this boy: nothing and no one.

'Hey baby... it doesn't matter. I'm here for you instead. I love you more than any mother could, we were meant for this to be.' I hugged him hard, never wanting to let go. I wish he thought I was mom; no one would ever notice the difference. He hugged back weakly, I knew that something was wrong, but I also knew that he would be playing at the children's park soon enough, and he would soon forget this conversation. We walked over a beautiful bridge as the fog slowly came in, brushing softly on our faces. The air chilled us, but we were both prepared for the weather, sea weather

was always unpredictable. The mist started to collect on the cobble stone as we entered the gates of the park.

'Go play.' I said as he ran towards the playground and I sat on an old cast iron bench. There was no one else playing, we were abandoned in the middle of nowhere. The sounds of small boats being hit by waves and the bump up against another boat was the only sound we heard. I looked for Marcello, he sat alone on the highest point of the small playground, looking down, deep in thought.

The weather had made up its mind.

'You're what?' Connie's voice echoed through the house, as she spoke in excitement.

'Shhh, keep it down.' Jen had been resting in bed for the last two days, and she wanted out. Every time she thought that she could leave her room, Adam was right there escorting her back to bed, mumbling something about 'doctor's orders.' Gladly, Connie decided to make a surprise visit and give her verity from her lonely, death threatening thoughts.

'Don't worry about school; Mr. Jenks completely understands.' Connie sat at the edge of the bed trying to comfort her friend.

'I haven't even thought about it. My whole life feels like it is going to change.'

'It probably will, but I'm sure Adam will always be here for you whenever you need it.'

Connie looked at her friend. *She doesn't look too good, I don't think she's telling me everything.* Her face was still as pale as the night she left the art show, her face seemed sad almost as though she was giving up.

'Mr. Moretti came in yesterday. He wanted to see your presentation, but he was equally impressed by your work. He even asked Mr. Jenks if he could buy a piece. Ironic, isn't it?' Connie didn't even leave enough time for Jen to respond before she continued. 'Rumor has it that Mr. Jenks ask if you want to study in Italy with Mr. Moretti, is that true? God, Jen, can you imagine if it were? That would be the best experience of your life, not to mention how incredibly handsome he is. Not that that would matter, apparently he is engaged. All the good ones are taken aren't they? Jen, don't look so down. I think that you will make a good mother. Oh, I was going to ask, who was the guy that answered the door? Man, you are always surrounded by good looking men. Is he taken?'

It took a moment for Jen to register that Connie had finished speaking. Connie's energy level was always high, normally Jen could handle it, but today she was just too exhausted. A stinging sensation took place behind her eyes, making her tear up and quickly close her eyes. Jen tried to hide her pain.

'So he liked my paintings?'

'Who... oh yes he did.'

'He can take one if he wants.' Her tears could hide no longer.

'You will be working with him shortly though, won't you?' Connie's energy changed. There was something wrong. 'Jen, baby, what's going on?'

It took a moment before Jen could even gain control of her voice.

'I'm not going to Italy, Connie. I can't go now.'

'Maybe things are still possible. It will only be a few months, by then you could come back, and you still will be able to get ready to have a child.'

'Connie... I don't think its possible, I am too sick.'

'Jen, sweetheart, having a child isn't being sick.' Connie wanted to laugh but she knew that Jen really didn't look well.

'Hey Jen, when you want to talk, you know where to reach me. But now, I think it is time for you to sleep.' Connie hugged her friend good-bye and Jen rolled over to go to sleep. By the time Connie was out the door, Jen was asleep.

The colours of the sky seemed to melt into the waters of the Agratic Sea. Today the clouds drifted in the distant sky and the sun came out to shine through even the darkest canals. The city was just getting ready for the day. She stood on a familiar balcony, a place she felt comfortable.

When she touched the stone, however, she felt nothing, almost disconnected from the place she was in. The only sensation she felt on her skin was the heat of the sun, which seemed to get warmer and warmer as the moment drifted on. Behind her she felt someone wrap his arms around her. She took his hands, unquestionably, pressed them to her so she could feel every part of them. She turned her face toward the man, but as she looked back the sun caught her eyes and all she saw was a bright nothing. As her eyes cleared she realized she lay in her bed and it was the morning sun that interrupted her dream. It was only a dream.

It felt senseless to be waiting in bed resting, it seemed to create nothing but turmoil in her head. She lifted herself to sit up in her bed. Beside her on the side table sat a fresh breakfast of toast, fruit and orange juice. She smiled as she thought about how thoughtful Adam was and how much he cared for her. This time when she woke up everything felt much better, she felt refreshed, the cramping in her abdomen had calmed down.

A slight knock on the door and with no hesitation it opened.

'Good morning.' It was Tom standing at the edge of the room with a jar of jam. There was a silence. Jen said nothing, her brain froze at his sight. Tom was able to continue. 'Strawberry jam, sorry there was no raspberry left.' He stood locked with Jen's eyes. A million words and nothing to say.

'Are you going to come here and hug me, or what?' Jen laughed spreading her arms out for Tom to fill them. There was no hesitation in his steps from the door to the bed. When their bodies came together, fully embraced in a tight hug, it felt right for the both of them.

'I wish you would have never left.' She whispered as her chin rested on his shoulder. 'Why did you leave?'

'You have Adam.' Tom struggled to answer - he never wanted to leave her.

'I know, but you had me.'

Tom pulled back. She was being honest so it was time for him to reciprocate. 'I couldn't watch Adam take you away from me. I was falling in love with you.'

Jen tried to stand up but faltered for a second, Tom swiftly moved to help her. 'It's alright. I'm okay.'

'You'll never know Jen, you will never know.' He wanted to hold her and tell her everything, tell her who Adam was, let her know that it was Adam who took her life away... but he stopped. She had already gone through too much.

'Yes, I do know.' Tom was thrown off guard more than anything as Jen spoke. 'I know how you feel. I wish you would have stayed.' Jen didn't know where all of this was coming from. 'Adam... I love him, he is absolutely amazing. But when he came back... it was only you I thought about. It took me a long time.' Jen stopped and took hold of Tom's hand. 'I'm sorry, I shouldn't have told you this... it's too late now, life has changed. Tom, I am so glad to see you.'

They both knew that life was now different, but there was still the knowledge in both of them of what they once wanted.

'Adam must be so happy that you are here, he needs friends like you.'

'Jen...' There was so much left unsaid. *Change the subject.* '...don't forget to eat, Adam told me that you have hardly ate anything since you got out of the hospital.

'Thank you!' Jen sat on the edge of her bed as she ate the contents on the plate. 'How long are you here for? I would love for you to stay awhile.'

'Actually, I leave tonight... I am going out of town for some work.'

'Oh. I see. As long as you promise to come back.'

'I will, sooner than you think.' Tom started to walk away.

'Tom, I hope that you understand.'

Without turning around, Tom took a deep breath. 'You have nothing to worry about, just know how amazing you are.' And with those words, once again, he walked away from her.

Old Moment

Chapter Twelve

I placed my arms softly around Angelo's neck. He sat in the same chair and I would always come up behind him, feeling the stubble on his neck, loving every part of him.

'Love, your painting is amazing. So beautiful and free.'

'This is not mine.' His voice seemed deeper then normal, but welcoming all the same.

'Where did you get it?' It looked so much like his, I couldn't tell the difference in the style.

'It is one of the students. I cannot stop looking at it. I know this piece, I have seen it before.'

'Did you ask him what his thought was when he painted this?'

'No, I did not get to meet her, she was supposed to do a presentation but she was ill. She is the student I asked to come and study under me.'

A spark of jealously filled my blood. I couldn't help but know that he would be intrigued by her more than what I had to offer. I had nothing to give him, nothing but myself.

'Kate, look at this, it looks like my mother's dining room. Here we all are... my mother, sisters, baby Marcello and you.' Angelo stood up, never taking his eyes off of the painting. I looked closer. The faces were murky and unclear, but I knew one thing, that it was not myself sitting in that spot next to baby Marcello. It was not me it was Jen.

The shop had never been so full of paintings; Angelo had never felt so inspired since Jen had left. It was this painting that he took from the school. He had never seen this work or style before. It was his, but almost better. It was more raw and rustic looking the technique was not quite there, but Angelo knew it wouldn't take her long. She was brilliant.

Painting had become Angelo's life, that and his little boy. He could never love anyone more than Marcello. Angelo continued, every day, to imagine what his life would be like if Jen hadn't disappeared. He didn't know if he wanted to be angry at her for leaving, or love her even more, because he couldn't see her. Sometimes it was hard, and today was one of those days. Marcello was almost five years old, yet the questions of his mother came more and more.

'Papa?' Marcello came into Angelo's shop.

'Si, Marcello?'

'Why has mother not come back?'

It had been almost five years since his mother had left, but it would be a lifetime to forget about her.

' I am not sure, Marcello.' Angelo tried to hide his frustration and turned to look at his painting. 'That is something I will never know.'

There was a long moment of silence. Marcello looked up and tried not to cry. 'I hate her.'

'Marcello... do not talk like that. I never wish to hear that come from your mouth again.' Angelo stood in anger.

'She left me, she never wanted me. She left me and she's never coming back.' Marcello started to cry, no longer being able to hold it back.

Angelo held him tight. 'You have many people that love you more than anything else in the whole world, Kate loves you and I love you, we will never let anything happen to you.'

'Angelo,' Kate stood at the loft above them. 'The phone is for you.'

'Grazie.' Angelo rushed upstairs, taking the phone with him to the other room. Kate traded spots with Angelo and went downstairs to be with Marcello. She sat where Angelo always sat when he looked at his paintings for hours.

'Marcello... do you want to paint?' Kate said with excitement trying to change the mood that Marcello wore so heavily on his face.

'No. Can I play with my plane?' His mood changed at the thought of his plane, his eyes lit up and he took off to his room.

Kate stayed, trying to sit in Angelo's mind. Waiting for Angelo, wondering if he was going to make another sale. The amount of paintings that were displayed out in front of her was absolutely amazing. Angelo had become engulfed in his work, almost like a man who went deranged. Kate would wake up in the middle of the night to the sound of him moving in his shop. Looking down to him she would find him painting, all his work completed in the moonlight and nothing else.

Today, as she sat on his chair, she noticed the vision of how brilliant his art had become. He was the master he had always wanted to be, and Kate was there to support him.

At the back of his shop he kept his older paintings covered. Kate had always stayed away from that area. Without words, she knew that the area was not to be touched. She always thought that one day Angelo would show her what was underneath the white sheets. Maybe it was a surprise, a painting just for her as a gift for their wedding.

Something, today, triggered her curious mind. Today, she let her curiosity out of its cellar, and without recalling how it happened, she made her way toward the uncharted territory; the back of the studio.

One, *Kate stops in front of the painting.* Two, *she reaches her hand out to grip the white sheet.* Three, *she softly pulls the white sheet away.* Four, *the reveal.* Five, *the reaction.*

Kate's body froze for what seemed more than a moment. Her curiosity could not help her now. There was nothing to take back the moment. The slight smile that was once on her face of sweet curiosity now turned into a salty tear.

Kate wanted to reach out to the painting. It was her; the woman that haunted her thoughts. A haunting was just as strong in the day as it was in the night. There she lay perfectly beautiful. *I wish I could be her.* Kate could not take her eyes away from the masterpiece. The jealousy collected in her throat, questions raced through her mind. *When did Angelo paint that? Why does he still have it?*

Jen was a goddess, maybe not to the rest of the world, but to Angelo she was a goddess and Kate saw that in the moment. Kate followed the line of her ankles to her legs, hips, breasts, neck and face. Jen belonged in Venice. All the woman painted in Venice would live to make Venice the way she had become. The time when Venice was thriving and at the age of its resurrection, she was perfection. Kate could not compare in beauty. Here she stood, her shapeless skinny body, her thin, tangly hair and her little beady eyes. The painting soon became blurred through the swelling of her own tears. She could not even compare. She reached out to feel the painting, imagining that she could feel the softness of her skin, but the moment was taken away from her.

'KATE!!?!' The alert stern voice of Angelo made Kate jump, pulling her hand back and facing reality. She almost felt guilty as though it was her that betrayed his trust. She refused to look at him as he quickly made his way to her. Each step was quick, heavy and felt full of anger. Kate felt the shiver of goosebumps travel up her back as he approached her. Angelo never turned to look at her or notice the tears that would not stop. He pulled the white sheet that had fallen to the ground back over the painting, never taking a quick glance at the painting as though it were the plague.

Kate felt paralyzed as she saw the bright red appear in Angelo's skin, his anger streaming through him. With no more than a dart of eyes toward her, Angelo stormed away from her even faster than her arrived.

'Angelo!!?!' Kate tried to yell across the room, but came out as a crack, her voice full of sadness. The name lingered in the air, expecting an answer which never received a response. Angelo paused, but kept his head down as he opened the door and slammed it behind him.

Kate was left there with nothing and everything to say. She fell to the ground melodramatically. Softly she cried, pulling the sheet once again to expose the painting. A deep breath, and a longing to be someone else, she spoke softly: 'Leave me alone.'

Angelo's first response was to storm away. Just walk away from everything, *in this moment.* There, always in the back of his mind and the forefront of his heart he could not let Jen go. Angelo sat in the Vaporetto, replaying the first moment he ever met her, the pain she was going through, the grace she endured. Back at this moment, anger and sadness filled his blood. He just needed to know what happened to the woman that made him want to paint again. Nothing would stop him. However, there were limitations, as soon as she left he stopped painting. Emotions were connected with his ability or sometimes his lack of.

The Vaporetto was moving around in the water more than usual; the strong winds added life to the water. Angelo looked in disgust back at Venice. *'Stop eating me.'* he said out loud, no one else was in range to hear. It was obvious to him that something in Venice had died for him. This was no longer a place of romance, this was never a place of romance, it was a disguise. Venice *is* the place people go to die. Angelo saw it that moment, Venice silently asked him to leave.

'Si.'

He was facing reality! The only question: what *is* real? There was no one telling him. Angelo was hit with a feeling he never felt before, a feeling of having no home. He knew the base of that feeling started with that phone call. He had been waiting for that call all week. Waiting to find out when the student was on her way. Waiting for the moment to meet the young artist who painted his story.

When he answered that phone call, it was Mr. Jenks, and the way he spoke turned a gut in his stomach.

'Yes Angelo, how are you?'... 'I've got news for you'...

The student was no longer coming, something about her being sick, and needing a break. Something about a child, and birth complication... a whole group of excuses.

'Jen isn't doing well.' Mr. Jenks stated before the story.

Angelo kept replaying those words over and over; 'Jen isn't doing well' .... 'Jen isn't doing'... 'Jen.' This was his chance. This was his closure. It was her, there was no question. Something came back from that Art Show, had he heard that name? *Jen*. The similarity between their styles as artists, the name. Angelo believed in *destino,* and this was a vision that worked its magic. When he came from that life changing phone call, a stream of excitement bolted through his nerves. As he walked down the stairs back to his shop, the painting of Jen was right there in front of him. *It was her.* And as Angelo sat in silence, almost lifelessly in the vaporetto, he came back to reality. Venice was telling him '*salutare*' and he knew what was going to do. It was his turn to leave Venice.

***

It had been a couple days since Kate had pulled the sheet away from the painting. Only a couple days yet it felt as though it had been a couple months. Although she felt anger for Angelo, she held it back and wanted make sure that Angelo was not angry at her. She needed a resolution to this hanging event.

After Angelo stormed away from her, he hadn't returned home until later the next night. She was left alone with only her thoughts to keep her going, and it was those thoughts that she needed to be rid of. When Angelo finally returned, his answers were short and his eyes steered away from reality.

Kate sat alone at the tiny table in their undersized kitchen, and for a lack of anything better to do, polished the shabby old silverware. Her thoughts were full of contradictions. She wanted to get away, perhaps go to the market, however she wanted to be near him. She was waiting for the moment that he would come into the kitchen and wrap his arms around her, anticipating the moment.

In and out of the kitchen Marcello would come flying around with his plane, making sure he stopped the plane to make sure that Kate had time to board the plane, and then fly away again. It was little Marcello that always made Kate smile. She would never let him out of her sight, there was always in her a gut feeling that something would just take him away. She buried the feeling deep inside her and tried to let it go.

Kate lost track of time as she polished the silverware, it was not until she started polishing the same forks over for the second time that she started to feel the cramping in her hands.

'Kate...!' Marcello ran into the kitchen excited as a little boy at Christmas. 'Are you coming too?' Marcello started tugging on Kate's sleeve.

'Going where?'

'To Canada, where dad was before.' *A dagger hard in the abdomen.*

'Marcello,' Kate started to laugh, it was a joke he was playing. It couldn't be real. 'You are trying to trick me.' Kate started to tickle him, trying to divert his thoughts. His laughter hid the sound of Angelo's footsteps.

'No he's not joking.' Angelo stood at the entrance leaning on the wall.

Kate looked up and smiled. 'We are going to Canada...' She jumped up trying to hold in all her excited emotions. 'Are you serious?' There was no smile on his face. 'Angelo, what is it?'

Angelo stepped forward and embraced Kate. He took a quiet moment before he spoke. 'Marcello and I are going, we will only be gone for a short time.'

Kate's arms dropped and she let go of Angelo, her face filled with pain and sadness. She stepped back looking directly into Angelo's eyes, hers were full of questions.

'Marcello and I will go. When we get back we will go to your home... it has been too long since you have been away. We want to see your home.'

It took a moment, or even longer, the emotions of up and down, up and down continued. Kate couldn't decipher her feelings, she had questions but nothing came out of her mouth.

'Kate, when we go back to your home, I would like for us to get married.' Angelo smiled, it hid his pain. He knew that something could change, but he wanted to see Kate happy at that moment. And he saw it through the change of her expression on her face and in her body. Her happiness overwhelmed her and she started to cry and smile; once again she embraced Angelo. She put her confusion to the side.

Within a few hours they had it all figured out. Angelo was going back to see if he could find Jen, he would be there for only three days. He would take Marcello to show Jen what she left behind. Marcello would not know what was happening, not until he saw her. He couldn't get the little boy's hopes up, not unless he knew for sure. Kate would stay in Venice, not knowing Angelo's intent and she would get them ready to leave for Australia. She had to let her family know, the family she hadn't seen in years. Although she knew she would never say it out loud, she really did miss them.

When Angelo and Marcello left back to Canada, Kate never wasted a moment - she had a lot of work to do.

A Ring

Chapter Thirteen

I could only see him from a distance; however, it felt that he could not see me. My heart felt like it was going to jump out of my chest. My ears had a high pitch ring so loud I could hardly hear anything around me. It was outside in the hot sun. I looked directly at the sun for a second and spent the next moment trying, once again, to focus on him, the man I was about to marry. I held up my long flowing dress and couldn't help but wonder what she would have looked like in the same dress. I knew that I was plain compared to her, but I no longer cared. I had more then I ever wanted: I had Angelo, I had Marcello, I had a dream of a life. I held my dress and walked forward. I took a deep breath feeling everything and feeling nothing at the same time. I looked only at him and didn't notice anyone that was there to witness the moment, it was only him. I saw him looking at me, he smiled as our eyes locked. He wanted me and only me. This is always what I wanted. This is the wedding of my dreams. Then, like in any dream, I woke up.

Everything had been planned and was ready to go. The only thing I had to wait for was the arrival of Angelo and Marcello. The time seemed to drag so slowly, I could no longer bare it. I tried to use up my time, but everything felt like a diversion. There was only one thing I had left to do and that was to call my family. Call them and let them know that I was coming home to see them and coming home to get married. They would never believe me. I wasn't sure whether they were going to laugh or cry. The thought of calling them was deafening, but it had to be done. I would never leave my family unlike that lost soul that left her own flesh behind. At that time I thought that there was no way she could actually know how much she hurt us, Angelo, Marcello and myself. I was right, she really did have no idea, but it was for a different reason than I had thought.

And just as it happened before...

'Jen, you are not strong enough yet.' Adam just wished he could lock her away until she had their baby. She was too head strong to know what was the best for her. Her spirit was wild and her heart needed to be free. There was something holding her back, but he knew it wouldn't be long.

'Adam, don't say that. I am just going for a few days. Connie will be with me the whole time.' Jen started to pull her clothes from the dresser and stuff them rapidly into her bag.

'Well... let me go with you then.'

'You know I can't ask you to do that, you have a lot of work to do and I really can't get in the way of that.' She kissed him to seal her point.

'But Connie... with her? She will only tire you out.'

'I need her... intense... support. I haven't seen my dad in two years and he needs me. I need to be there for him. I'm his only child and I haven't been there for him before, I need that to change.'

'I know Jen, but you have been pretty sick. I'm not going to sugar coat it, I love you and I am worried.' Adam embraced her, but she pushed away.

'Adam, you know that I can take care of myself. I talked to my doctor and she said that I am perfectly safe, and if I feel sick at any point I will go to the hospital. It has already been a few weeks since I have been feeling really ill. I am much better now. I think I am good enough to go back to school, I am falling so far behind.'

'Okay... but if anything happens, I mean anything you call me right away and if you don't call, me you better get Connie to call. You got that? Adam was stern with his voice but it only made Jen laugh.

'Yes of course.' She kissed his forehead and ran down the stairs to meet Connie.

'Can you let me drive you to the airport at least?' Adam followed after her.

'That you can do. Let's go, Connie.' They made their way out the door and to the car.

'Connie, you better take care of her.' Adam said as they drove to the airport.

'Yes sir.' She laughed. 'I will not let her out of my sight, nor will I allow her to eat unhealthy foods. I will report back to you at 1600 hours and make sure that she says 'I love you' at the end of every phone call.'

'Good soldier, well taught.'

Connie changed her stature and looked over to Jen. 'I would never let anything happen to her. You know that Adam.'

'Yes Connie, I trust you.' Adam put aside his doubt with Connie and knew that she would never let anything happen to her.

' Jeez, both of you. You are acting as though I am some sort of child. It is all good, don't worry.'

'Jen, I do not trust you however.' trying to make a joke of the situation. He looked over at the woman that he loved. *What if she ever found out? What if she just left me? She needs me.* Adam's obsession grew every day with Jen, the thought of losing her was almost unbearable. There was no option, it just couldn't happen. ' You better have a good time.'

'Don't worry, we will.'

Jen and Connie made it to the airport with time to spare. As Jen's plane took off, Angelo's plane landed. A moment in time, a moment in life that just once didn't work the way anyone thought it would.

Another plane that took off that day was one that only Adam knew about. It was Tom's plane going back to Italy, only this visit would be different. This job would be like no other: Tom would be going back to Italy to do one last job for Adam, the hardest job he would ever have to endure.

***

Connie stood behind Jen with her hand on Jen's shoulder. Tension filled the air. She could feel Jen vibrating, her whole body trembling trying to catch up with itself. The hardest part for Connie was knowing that she couldn't do anything to help her friend.

'Jen, it's going to be okay.' Connie whispered, very well knowing that there was no way that was going to be true.

'This wasn't supposed to happen', she spoke through her tears. 'I need to go in and say good-bye.'

Connie removed her hand, 'What do you want me to do Jen? Do you want me to come in with you, or should I wait outside? Whatever you want, darling.' Jen looked over at Connie, who smiled and embraced her.

'No, Connie. I have to do this alone.' Jen walked away from Connie and followed the doctor. The hospital happened around her, life and death happened around her. However, Jen concentrated on what was before her, preparing her mind and body.

The doctor had already explained the situation. Jen had the feeling that the only reason why he was still alive was to say good-bye to her. This would be the moment of knowing, the moment of enlightenment. Passing from one place to the next - hopefully it would be a better place.

Jen and Connie had waited at the Calgary airport for her father, but he never came. After five hours they both decided that they would rent a car and drive out to the mountains, off to Jen's home town. When one hears *one phone call can change the world* it happened at that point, somewhere between Calgary and Canmore, Alberta ,Canada, *ring, ring.... hello.* This phone call was sender unknown, why did she answer? Tanya, a friend of her father called to say the life changing words. *'He was in a car accident.'* It was not just a car accident it was Jen's father driving to pick them up and he never made it, it was her fault. This was not just a car accident, it was good-bye. Jen's heart sunk within her as she heard the news, Connie didn't know how to console, no one expected this.

Was this his drinking? He was supposed to stop. A sense of guilt rushed through Jen as she thought about how she hadn't been around for him in his moments of need. *I am so sorry.*

When Jen received a call from her dad telling her that he needed to see her, she never questioned anything. She needed to be with him. When she stepped off the airplane and he wasn't there something inside of her started to feel ill.

'Jen...' The doctor took her out of her trance and brought her back to a place between life and death.

'Sorry.' *Where was she?*

'Jen... there is something I must tell you...' *Don't sugar coat it.* 'Your father is suffering from a tumor, when a person has a tumor in the brain they start to loose certain function, and in some cases it has people doing things that they can't recall.'

'Wait, what are you saying? Are you telling me that he is in an accident because of this?' Her legs started to shake and feel weak, *stay up, don't fall.*

'Yes, the accident was a result of this.' The doctor put his hand on the door knob getting ready to walk in.

'Wait, please, how long did he know this?' Jen demanded, trying to hide her frustration. 'How long?'

'About a year and a half.'

'No one ever told me?'

'He never wanted to bother you... is how he said it.'

No more waiting. 'I need to see him. Suddenly everything changed in Jen. She dreaded to see him before. She was nervous and scared before but in a snap that changed. He must of felt, yet he was all alone, that he never could tell her anything. She should have been there for him, she should have been taking care of him. Watching after him driving him where he needed to go. All these mixed feelings flying through through her mind, stopping at one; guilt.

The doctor opened the door revealing her father, weak and static on the hospital bed. Instant emotions freed in the locked tears in her eyes. She couldn't help but rush forward to his side. She saw right through the bandages and bruises, she saw right through the amount of weight he lost and how much he aged. In front of her was her father.

'Hi, dad.' There was no response. She took hold of his hand, held on tight.

'I will let you be with him.' The doctor stepped out of the room.

'Dad, I never knew, I'm so sorry.' She silently sobbed, knowing fully that he couldn't hear her, but knowing that her words needed to be said. ' I wish you would have told me, I would have dropped everything, I would have been right here for you. I should have known that something wasn't right.' Jen stopped, only for a moment to wipe away the flowing tears. 'I'm so sorry, Dad. I haven't been here for you. I want to let you know how much I love you. I always felt...' the words started to break up. 'I always felt that I took mom away from you and that it was my fault that you lived with as much pain as you do. If I could take back time, I would give up my life so that Mom could come back and be with you.'

'Don't even think that way.', a weak voice came from him.

'Daddy? It felt as though Jen was turning into a child, going back to a childhood that she never lived through - the childhood she always wanted.

'If I have ever made you feel that way, I want you to know that I never meant it.' He squeezed her hand with little strength as his words slowly, and with great difficulty, came out.

Jen had forgotten herself within her emotions; he could tell.

'Jenny, darling... it will be okay.' It was now her father consoling her. 'My only regret is that I wasn't a better father.'

'No, Dad. Please, it doesn't matter. I love you.'

'You look different, darling. Have you been feeling okay?'

'Dad, I should be asking you that.' She trailed her free hand down to her abdomen. 'But if you are asking... I'm pregnant.'

'What? I'm going to be a grandfather. Jen when did you find out? I have been waiting for this.' His excitement was there but his voice could hardly portray it as it became weaker and weaker.

'It was only a couple of weeks ago. But I was really sick so I have been locked away in my room. I was excited to tell you.'

'You are going to be a mom.'

Silence.

'Jenny?'

'Yes Dad?'

'I want to let you know that for me the most important thing... was you.'

Jen started to laugh through her tears. 'Dad, don't be so corny.'

'Jenny, a child and the connection you have with it is the most amazing feeling you will ever feel.' His voice was starting to completely disappear.

'Dad, maybe you shouldn't talk.' Jen stood up. 'I will get the doctor. You need something to drink.'

'No, Jenny. Sit down, it's okay. I want you to know that whatever happens I will always love you. I always have even if I never knew how to show it.'

'I love you too, Dad.'

'But...', he continued, '...a father wants to see his daughter happy. You are looking for something Jen. I want you to find it, and Jenny I don't know what it is you are searching for, but you do.' Jen sat back down again. There was another silence. He was right, she just could not believe it was real.

'Dad?'

'Yeah?'

'Why didn't you ever tell me that you were sick?'

'It wasn't important.'

'But Dad...'

'Jen... you know why. You are worth too much to me.'

The door opened slowly as the doctor came in.

'Jen, I think your father needs his rest. He has a big day ahead of him.'

'Okay.' She looked back into her fathers eyes. 'I will be seeing you. I love you. Don't forget that, kay?'

'I love you too, Jen. Good-bye.'

Jen bent over and kissed him on his cheek, too afraid to touch anything other than that. 'Don't say good-bye, I will see you soon.'

'Good-bye.' He whispered. Once again, her tears became fluid as the doctor escorted her out.

Connie stood close by when she came out of the hospital room.

As soon as the door closed behind them, Jen spoke both to the doctor and Connie, 'He knows he's going to die, I wonder what he feels right now.'

***

Angelo stole a deep breath from the fresh air as he left the airport once again, only this time he had a different mission, Marcello was by his side, completely oblivious on how close he was to meeting his real mother. The sun was already setting, the colors were different here than they were back home. It seemed to have softer, more blended colors of soft pinks, oranges and yellows. Angelo knew that they would have to wait until tomorrow to talk to Mr. Jenks

and find this mystery student. The thought of waiting made his heart beat faster and his mind race through the million possible outcomes.

The last few years Angelo questioned why she would have left every single day. Not once had Angelo stopped at the thought that she would have left Marcello and hismself on purpose. Angelo looked over at the little boy. *There is a reason why your with me.* Angelo said this in his mind every time he looked at this little boy. There was a reason why everything happened the way it did. Without even thinking otherwise, Angelo took in Marcello as his son. He knew that one day he would have to tell Marcello the truth. However, he kept delaying it to the point that he no longer knew if he could ever say anything.

As Angelo and Marcello waited for the morning time, it seemed to slip away into the abyss never to be seen again. *Tick, tock, tick tock.* The sun rose and the world woke up.

Angelo brought Marcello with him when he finally stepped up and decided to go see Mr. Jenks at the school. The day was a standard school day, mid spring waiting for the semester to end. Every student would be present. Inside that building once the door was open, Angelo had a chance of seeing her, her beauty taking over the rest of the class, the feeling overwhelming.

Before he knocked on the class door he took a deep breath in and noticed that Marcello did the same thing. It was the first time that Angelo noticed that Marcello was taking on the same feeling of excitement and nervousness.

Mr. Jenks opened the door to the classroom. It was a surprised shock more than anything else. In front of him the artist for Italy. *What an honor to have him back.*

'Everyone, we have our wonderful guest back.' He waved Angelo and little Marcello into the classroom. As soon as Angelo was made present to the rest of the class there was a large applause, made louder by the echo in the building. Marcello's chest rose and held his chin high. He was proud of his father. Angelo's attention was fully focused on finding her, looking carefully over every student, no reaction to the applause. One by one he eliminated the faces until there was no one left. His heart sank, but he didn't lose the hope that she still existed. The Jen Mr. Jenks was talking about was his Jen, there was no doubt in his mind. Everything happened for a reason.

'Mr. Moretti, I would love to ask you to stay and help me with my class, but I know that you are probably a little busy.'

'No, I am not, I would love to stay. As long as my son can stay as well.' The women in the class all made that little sighing noise and the men all laughed at their reaction. Marcello had won over their hearts.

'Mr Jenks, could we paint his son instead?' One of the girls at the back of the classroom shouted out, hoping they could paint him instead of the dead pig carcass that sat at the front of the classroom.

'I think that is up to him.' Mr. Jenks looked at Marcello and then up to Angelo in a hopeful request.

Angelo never had to answer, it was Marcello who piped up and said, 'I would be honored.'

As the class went by, Marcello sat patiently without moving as everyone set their eyes on him. Angelo, on the other hand, wasn't patient. He thought about Jen, who wasn't there. She felt so close yet so far away. He talked to Mr. Jenks who told him that she would be at home. She had taken a short leave from school, some issues had come up. When Angelo openly asked where Jen lived, Mr. Jenks never questioned his motive and told him with directions.

As soon as Angelo found out where she lived, he wanted to ditch out of the class and see her after so many years, years that moved slowly without her. There was no way this was not his Jen, no way. He was so close. Instead he stayed and helped the students find the right vision that they were looking for.

As soon as the class finished, Angelo was the first one to take off, promising Mr. Jenks that he would allow him to take them out for dinner. Marcello, with pride, bowed to the rest of the class and they clapped for him, feeding his little boy ego.

How Angelo made it from the class room to in front of her door he did not know. But suddenly he found himself standing there, not recalling if he had already knocked. After a few passing moments with no answer, Angelo softly knocked, waiting... *waiting, wondering, hoping.*

Marcello paid no attention as he sat at the end of the walk way playing with his plane. Finally what seemed like eternity ended. A man answered the door. Angelo vaguely recognized him, but didn't know why. *Who was this man?* A streak of jealousy hit through Angelo, a streak he never even realized he ever had. And if Angelo thought that he recognized him, this man definitely recognized Angelo. A moment of silent awkwardness wasted by.

'Hello.', the strange man said, as though he was caught off guard.

'Hello, my name is Angelo.'

'Yes, I know who you are. Angelo Moretti. I met you at the art show. My name is Adam.' Adam's heart started racing. *What was he doing here? Did Tom release something and screw up? Or maybe Tom did this on purpose, because he was jealous? Tom could never hide it that well. Stay cool, continue to breathe.*

'Hello, Adam.' Pause. 'I'm looking for Jen.' His hands started to get clammy and his body started to betray him.

'Oh...' *Is this relief or is this worse?* 'I see, she's actually not here. She is on the other side of the country, her father just died.'

'I'm sorry to hear that.' *Disappointment.* He wasn't sure if he was more sorry that she was absent or that her father just passed away.

'I can pass on a message for you.' Adam just wanted him to leave. That painting that Angelo Moretti painted of a goddess, that goddess that looked identical to Jen, would not leave his mind. ' How do you know her?' Not really wanting to hear the answer.

'From the school.' *Did that sound believable?*

'I see, do you have a message?' Adam seemed to get a little irritated and looked away. In the short distance was a little boy playing with an airplane, how he had not noticed the boy earlier was a mystery. His breath almost stopped. That was Jen's child there was no doubt in his mind. The words of Dr. Engle suddenly came clear to him, that child at the end of the walk way was Jen's. The boy had the same eyes. Adam saw this and his mind almost collapsed. Jen could never know about this. Adam needed them to leave, he was going to pretend this never happened. It only took him a second to make up his mind.

'No you do not need to leave a message.' Angelo tried to hide his sadness. 'I was wondering if I could see a picture of her?'

What an odd question. *Think quickly*. Adam just couldn't say 'no.' If he said no this man would be too suspicious, if he said 'yes', it couldn't be a real picture of Jen. *Think quickly.* 'Yes, just one second.' Adam left for a moment and came back with a picture. 'Here she is.'

This was the moment of truth for Angelo. He wanted nothing more than to see a picture of her. He took hold of the picture. When he allowed his eyes to focus on the person in front of him, all hope inside him disappeared, the women in the picture was not the Jen that he was looking for. The disappointment inside him was far too great to hide. He slowly handed back the picture.

'Thank you, sorry to bother you.' Angelo started to leave before Adam could say good-bye. Adam closed the door and breathed out a sigh of relief. Connie to the rescue.

Angelo walked away not knowing that he had been deceived. With no hope left in his blood it was now the right time to let Jen go. He took hold of Marcello's hand and left back to Venice that night, forgetting about his dinner plans with Mr. Jenks. The flight was too long to be left with his thoughts. He had a lot of preparation to do with his future wife, then off to Australia as promised.

Marcello and Angelo arrived back home moments before he would receive a phone call from the Venizia Polizia - they had found Jen's body. It had been found lifeless in a canal, and it had been there for a while. The next day Angelo would go down to the police station to verify the corpse. Her body was deteriorated, her face completely gone, but her beautiful birthmark was still there, always there. Angelo was the only one to verify that it was her. Rest in Peace.

His Hesitation

Chapter Fourteen

The wedding was cancelled, instead it was replaced with a funeral. No matter what everyone said, I never believed it. That body was not Jen's. They had no proof that it was her, aside from the birth mark that Angelo remembered. Once again, Jen came back to haunt me. This day was the day that was going to be a dream come true. A beautiful dream. I should have been able to feel the hot Australian sun on my shoulders. I should have been kissing his soft lips and making love to him for the first time. However, all of this changed. When Angelo told me to wait off on the wedding, I wanted to cry, but instead, I stood my ground, regretting most of what I said, but knowing that was needed.

'Angelo, I'm going home. Come when you are ready to marry me. I need you in my life, but I need you to be settled first.' I gave him a long hug and kissed him on his cheek.

'Thank you for understanding, Kate.' Angelo hugged her tightly. 'I will come for you, I promise you that.'

And with those words, I left him. Never wanting to, but knowing at the moment it was for the best. I needed him to love me, I would never ask him to love me nearly as much as he loved her, but I need some of it. This time I would go by myself, and more than anything, I would miss Marcello.

'Are you going to tell him?' I wanted to know before I left.

'No, not yet. I will tell him when he is older.'

I said 'alright' back, but wished that he would tell Marcello the truth about his mother.

Tom only had to do this one last job and then he would go home, wherever home was. When he left back to Italy he wanted to curse Adam for making him go through with this. This would be his last and one of his most difficult jobs, but he still did it.

Finding a body that most closely resembled Jen, aging its death time, and making it almost completely impossible to identify. It was a hard job, placing it where it could be found was another.

Why Adam had Tom do this particular job, Tom would never know. It was not just a coincidence that this artist lived in Italy and painted a picture of Jen. Tom could break down and tell this mysterious artist what happened. They must have been together before Jen's accident. Adam wanted to kill off the old Jen and make sure that this artist, Angelo Moretti, would forget her from his life.

Tom's last job was to find that painting and steal it. It had taken him a few days to locate the painting, it was in a studio that also duplicated as Angelo Moretti's home on the Island of Guideccia. After Angelo left the Police Station, Tom followed him home. And for the last couple days he had watched him continuously.

There was one complication, one that Tom never expected. However, the more he thought about it, the more it made sense. With Angelo came a little boy. There was no questioning it. The boy belonged to Jen. Tom knew that Adam had taken this child away from Jen. The child even looked like Jen. The second that Tom saw the boy, he had to leave, he went back to the hotel room and started to cry. He was torn, he wanted to tell Jen everything, but the other side of him thought that it would be too painful for her. That's when Tom decided to never tell her anything - it wasn't his job. If anything, it was Adam's job to put together what he had undone.

It was three in the morning and the City of Canals slept silently for Tom to sneak around in. The plan would work well. Tom rented a small boat with high speed in case he needed a quick getaway. The back of Angelo's warehouse was the best spot to hide the boat. On the second level of the house was where he would make an entrance. The kitchen had a large window that Angelo always left open a crack, enough where Tom could easily break into. He would then travel down the stairs to his studio and only take one painting. Angelo kept it at the back of the studio where it was the only one covered by a clean white sheet, all the others were covered by old dirty sheets.

It was that easy. And there Tom stood ready to reveal the painting. He had been silent almost non existent, and was very proud of his ability.

The sheet swiftly came off. Tom lost his breath. In front of him was Jen there was no question there was no one more beautiful in his mind. He had never seen her like this. She was at peace with herself, truly content. Since Tom had met Jen, there was never a settled feeling within her. Tom was surprised that Adam was ever able to lock Jen down. She was a free spirit and nothing could tame her.

'Go ahead, take it.' A quiet voice came from some other place in the studio. Tom almost fell over, what went wrong? How did he know that he would be there? Tom had no idea how long he was staring at her. Had he lost track of time? This part was not supposed to happen. Tom turned behind him after a moment of letting his eyes adjust. There he was, Angelo sat in the shadows, noticeably in turmoil. He had not been taking care of himself. Tom didn't know how to react, he had become a deer trapped in headlights.

'Go ahead, take it.' His voice seemed to slur as though he had been drinking. 'She's gone, you know. Take it. There's nothing left of her anyway.'

Tom stood there only for a moment.

'TAKE IT.' Angelo raised his voice. It was almost as though Angelo knew that Tom was coming. However, without hesitation, Tom grabbed the piece with great delicately and leisurely walked out of the front door not looking behind him.

His heart felt as though it were going to jump right out of him. The painter no longer held his posture, something inside of him had snapped. He looked crazed and drained of any energy he ever had. When Jen was alive to him, he held onto hope, but now it had departed. Apart of Tom wanted to console this man but there was nothing he could do.

Tom left in his boat, quietly, trying to figure out what just happened . He knew he would never speak of this again.

***

'Are you at least glad to be home?' Adam tried to hold onto Jen and embrace her. However, Jen kept walking away.

'I'm not sure where home is, Adam.' She kept herself from looking in his eyes, moving from room to room, cleaning her art projects up. It had been three weeks since Jen had last seen the place, a longer trip then she had expected. Three days turned into three weeks.

'Honey, baby... of course you have a home here. This is your home.' Adam had waited for the moment of her return, but he never expected a mass confusion in her mind to come after him. And by the looks of it neither did she.

'I know.' *Sad sigh*. 'It just feels like I don't belong any where. I just need to let go.' She finally just sat down, as though she ran out of things to do.

'Of course it's normal to feel that way...' he made his way closer to her, '...you have gone through a lot lately, having to plan a funeral for your father isn't an easy thing to do, and the delicate position that you are in.'

'I'm fine, the doctor says I'm fine.' Jen stood up again. 'I am so unsettled. I need to go somewhere.'

'Jen you just got back. You need to rest.'

'Adam, that's all I have been doing. I need to catch up with school and my life. I have been keeping it on hold.' Instead of staying away from him, this time she knew she needed to be held.

'Do what you have to do to feel as though you belong, but remember you have to take care of this.' Adam bent down and kissed her small belly that had grown since she had been gone. A child waiting to be born.

'I know, we will both be taking care of that.'

There was a pause, a silence that felt full of energy. No one needed to talk. Just be. Just being was one of the most difficult actions Jen could possibly act upon. To have such an unsettling feeling and yet just be could hardly co-exist with each other. Yet at this moment she was able to breathe in the exact second.

'I'm going to go to the studio. I won't be too long, I just need sometime to feel like I belong again.'

'No problem, babe.' Adam let go of her. 'I won't go anywhere.'

Jen left the house and walked casually to the studio. The weather left misty rain and a fresh smell in the air. It was as though God was softly washing her skin and cleansing her mind. Much had happened in these last few weeks. Her father stayed in her mind guiding her feelings and her ability to continue on. There was no question in her mind that he was leading her.

The walk to the studio made life feel as though it had meaning, even though Jen felt unsettled in her life she knew that one day she would conquer. She must have felt it before and she knew that she would feel it again. The journey of life. The existence of time. The portrait of content. The wonder of everything and the fulfillment in nothing. With that, Jen took a deep breath and stepped into a place of comfort, a place where she could be free and paint what lay within her.

This time she walked into the classroom, it was empty but it felt so full of life. Flick. She turned on the lights. Instantly her vision became distorted, and a shiver went through her mind. In front of her she saw what the other students had been working on in her absence. The boy that she dreamed of. Only this time there was many different interpretations, but all clearly the boy. A tear, almost instantly, ran down her face. 'Dad, what are you telling me?' Jen said softly. There was no one else to hear it besides the essence of her father. Jen closely studied each and every painting. Some painted with soft lines others were hard and jagged. Some lacked colours while others had too much.

Jen knew her painting well. Hers was not a painting, however, hers was real. Jen could reach out and feel the boy. This time when her hand touched his she felt a real connection, there was nothing to break it.

Replacing Yourself

Chapter Fifteen

This time it was real. She was gone from our lives, dead or not, the only traces left of her was Marcello. Marcello, however, was more than precious, and every moment spent with him was a blessing. He had just had his fifth birthday. I thought that I would miss his birthday, being home in Australia away from my little boy. The biggest surprise of my life came on Marcello's birthday: it was him. Angelo flew to my home with Marcello. He had come. It took only a few months for him to come to me. Every single day that I spent away from him, only made me want him more. I wanted to go back to him, but I held the painful feeling out. And as I prayed he came to Australia to find me. Right by his side was a little boy who jumped for joy when he saw me. My heart lifted at the sight of them, their silhouettes distinct and comfortable to me. Angelo had let her go, he had put that period of his life away and come to be with me.

This time it was real I walked down the aisle in the beaming Australian sun. Angelo looked down to me his smile melted my very existence. My family was watching, all of them wondering how it was possible that I was able to be with someone as good as Angelo.

I looked over the small crowd of people who were to witness our love for each other. As a surprise to his family Angelo had flown them all down to be with us, even his evil sister, Eleanora, who sat there with a grimace on her face the whole ceremony. Caprice, his mother, sat in a distant glance that appeared after she found out that I was no longer just the help but I was now with her son. But I overlooked all of them. In life it was now my turn, and this turn was more than I ever imagined.

When 'I do' was said, my whole life changed, everything inside of me grew stronger. I was where I wanted to be. Just like I always imagined the romance of Venice had actually come alive.

Marcello stood beside Angelo. He seemed happy enough yet something inside was not settled. He was too young of a boy to worry about where his real mother was. It was my turn now; I replaced his mother.

'Come on, Jen.' Connie sat at one side and Adam over Connie's shoulder, both of them encouraging her to push. *Breathe and push. Just breathe.*

'Connie, move out of the way, I need to be close.'

'So do I.'

'That is my child coming out of my soon to be WIFE.'

'That is *my* little niece coming out of *my* best friend.'

'Only by choice, we can easily change that.'

Jen could hear them both, but there was no way she could laugh at the two of them the pain seemed unbearable. She saw Connie and Adam right in front of her... as clearly as she saw them one moment, the next moment they were gone like fuzz going over her eyes, in and out of focus, in and out of pain. No longer in control.

Sensations started to change to her, the pain different from before. She lay back on a cold bench, her skirts lifted up to her thighs the cold air giving her a permanent chill. There stood a man she must have known in some space and time, in some life time. A man that looked worried, yet she felt comfortable and entranced by his eyes. *Everything will be alright.* Who was telling her this? Jen started to feel the sensation as though she was floating on the water. It soothed her, rocking her like a child ready to fall asleep.

Her eyes would not allow her to blink, she could not break the connection with the strange yet not so strange man looking down at her. He was her guardian angel. God had sent her an Angel - *thank you God.* Even in all her pain Jen found a moment to smile. Slowly the man disappeared and she was back in the hospital bed. Around her chaos, but inside her peace.

The man came back the floating sensation continued. *'Gabriel.'* she whispered, *the protector of Women and Children.*

'Angelo.' He smiled at her.

She lost his face from her mind. In front of her was blood, flashing lights and more chaos.

'Jen?!!! Jen!' Voices all over, voices everywhere. 'Can you hear us, Jen?' Shouting, screaming.

There he stood at the back of the room: Angelo. Her eyes focusing only on him. Oblivious to the people around her. Then there was darkness.

***

It had come in a small white package. There was no return address or any indication of what country the mail had come from. Angelo was the one to receive it, delivered from the post office. Instead of opening it right away like he wanted to, he left it on the kitchen table, increasing the suspension. He was in the middle of his painting, it needed to become complete. He wanted no distractions. He stood there, looking at the painting, watching it look back at him, looking at the bland colouring and wondered what he could do to fix it.

'I should just start over.' He thought about the student that was supposed to come and study under him. The student that never came. He could not teach anyone at the moment. The inspiration had flown away, loss and pain were what was left.

The news about his paintings had started to travel around the world. He needed to keep up with his buyers. Angelo spent most of this time traveling from Art Show to Art Show making fortunes he never expected. If only his father could see him now. Trying to catch up with the amount he was selling was starting to get difficult. He needed a break that would take up no time. *Impossible.*

Kate, without saying anything, was starting to get upset with the fact that Angelo was continuously leaving. She started to age and it had only been just over a year since they had been married, however this new found fame was hard on the both of them. But they continued as though nothing was happening. Silent and pretending.

An hour later after trying to get the colours right, Angelo took a break - something was off. That package was now on the forefront of his mind, the mystery waiting to be found.

Up the stairs Angelo went in the moment, one step at a time. Breathing in and out, when he reached the package he picked it up, slowly and deliberately he opened it. His hand slipped into the package. *Out comes the surprise.* Inside was a print of his stolen painting, it was her. He touched her. *Beauty.* On the back of the print was an imprint; *'Always immortal.'* Angelo stood still. *How could this be?* He stood still, lost in her. He cried. He would never be able to let her go. She broke him. *What was the reason without her?*

BANG, BANG, BANG! Angelo's attention was quickly pulled away from the picture. Someone anxiously wanted a quick response.

'What's going on?' Kate slowly emerged from the bedroom; she looked tired and upset.

Angelo looked over to her and back to the door. He never answered her question. Gripping tightly to the print he made his way to answer the noise.

BANG, BANG, BANG!

Angelo cautiously opened the door, nervous at its urgency. In front of him his eldest sister, Eleanora, flew right in. *Breathing too heavy, panicking heightens.* It took her a moment but she finally turned and looked at Angelo, her eyes crazed over, days of tears grew heavy on her.

'Eleanora, Eleanora... calm down. What is it?' Angelo's first thought was that something was wrong with one of his other sisters' or even his mother. Were the others in some sort of danger?

'Angelo, I am so sorry.'

Kate looked down at them, trying to understand what they were saying, but everything was going too fast. She stood watching, disappointed in her delay in learning Italian.

'Eleanora, slow down. What is it?'

'Angelo... the day that Jen left...' Pause. 'The day she left...it was my fault.'

'What do you mean?' *Stay calm.*

Eleanora distanced herself from her brother. She braced herself. There was this moment of empathy in Angelo, and they both looked at each other in deep care. Eleanora knew that with what she was about to say, she would never see that look again, she wanted to treasure it. 'I told her to leave.' *No taking those words back.*

'What?!' He could not filter his anger.

Eleanora started to cry all over again. 'I'm so sorry. I told her that she wasn't welcome. I never thought that she would actually leave. When she never came back I thought that it was by choice. I never once thought that she died.'

Angelo never wanted to hit a women before, but this time it took everything to hold that anger away from her.

'I wanted to tell you this, I wanted to say sorry the day it happened, but I could not. I never knew until it was too late that you actually loved her.'

'Why? Why did you tell her to go? Why?' Angelo started to pace back and forth, distracting him from his anger.

'Because... I did not think that she was good enough for you. I wanted you to stay in the house and live with us. The family needed you.'

Angelo started crying; he couldn't be strong anymore. He started weeping as though he was a child. He wanted to go back into time and change everything, but Jen was gone, he saw the proof with what was left of her body. She would never come back.

Eleanora came to try and comfort him, she could not see her brother like this. 'I could not hold the guilt in any longer. I am sorry, my brother.'

'One day I will find it in my heart to forgive you, sister, but right now I need you to leave.'

Without thinking otherwise, Eleanora left, hoping the day of his forgiveness would be soon. Angelo looked up at Kate, who stood, lost in confusion. She saw the same hurt in his eyes: it was her again.

***

'Jen, please... you have to stop going on these spontaneous trips.' Adam tried to hold her down on the bed, he wanted to stop her from leaving.

'Come on, Adam. I haven't left anywhere in years. I don't know what you are talking about.'

Gabriela giggled, pulling both of their attention over to the one year old darling child.

'What about Gabriela? You can't just leave her.'

'I won't, I am taking her with me.'

Adam knew his wife well enough to know that she wasn't going to give up, that no matter what she wasn't going to let him stop her. But she couldn't go, it was so easy to find his buried secret.

'But why Venice? You don't have good memories there.' Adam was thinking of anything, anything that would stop her from going.

'I need to go back. I need to pick up my things.'

'Jen, the bank said they would mail your belongings back to you that was left in the safe. It wouldn't take that long.'

'Adam please. I will only be gone one week. I promise you it will put my mind at rest. You know these thoughts have been bothering me for years I need to let go of them.'

'I know, it's just that I worry for you. I don't want you to get hurt. I wish you would let me go with you.'

'No, Adam, you know that I need to do this.' Jen rolled over to pick up Gabriela. 'I want to show her the place I died.'

He paused before he spoke. *Did she actually believe that?* 'You never died Jen.' Adam was at his last resort. There was nothing he could do to hold his wife back. The only thing he could do now was pray.

Ever since Jen gave birth to Gabriela, she could not get the image of that man nor the child from her mind. His eyes looked as though they knew better then any other person in the world. His name she remembered clearly: Angelo. She had only ever heard of that name once before - the name of the painter. For some reason, this was something that made complete sense in her life. The paintings matched her life. The man she saw could only be him. And so, she was going to Venice to find him and find some answers to all her questions. This information she hid from Adam.

All this led to her packing up and with Gabriela, leaving the very next day. When she arrived at the Marco Polo Airport, she had no idea where she was going. She knew that she wanted to go straight for Angelo Moretti's house. The address came from Mr. Jenks' desk, and conveniently dropped it into her bag. She wanted to take off right away, but she knew that she needed to find a place for her and little Gabriela. The little love of her life sleeping in her arms.

When she once again stepped into the City of Canals, unclear memories started to surface. She saw herself at a small cafe, holding her belly, full of worry. She saw herself running through the narrow streets, feeling the panic rise within her and she saw the peace that so long ago she had lost.

When Gabriela finally woke up, they were already comfortable in a hotel room that Jen felt she had seen before. Gabriela cried unsure of her surroundings, ready to be fed.

It was already later in the day by the time Jen built enough courage to show up sporadically at Angelo's door step. She found herself weaving around the old buildings on the island of Gudicecca and there she stood in front of his oversized door.

She stood, something kept her from knocking. Gabriela in one arm, she placed her hand on the door, something about this place felt undeniably recognizable. It was time to knock. The first knock was quiet and uncertain. She waited another moment. The second knock was loud and deliberate. There was an instant answer. In front of her, a surprised woman.

Kate couldn't believe her eyes. Here Jen stood in front of her, not alone either. In her arms, a young child. There she stood, even more beautiful then Kate remembered, even more graceful. What was more surprising to Kate was when Jen saw Kate, there was no reaction, not even a hint of familiarity.

'Hello.' Kate said slowly, almost wanting to physically push her away, but she too stood frozen at the door, trying to hide what she knew.

'Hello... my name is Jennifer Sipi. I was in the art class Angelo Moretti went to visit over a year ago, I happened to miss him because I was unwell. I would be very honored to meet him.' She felt like a young teenager not really sure what to say.

'You have never met him before?' Kate lost in her confusion. Was this some sort of joke? 'Have you ever been here?'

'No, I was in Italy once along time ago. I believe perhaps a few years ago, but I have no memory of it, some sort of accident.'

'Wow. What happened?' Kate was unsure how to react.

'I'm not sure.' Jen laughed, looking down at Gabriela who seemed to be making a strange noise. 'Nothing has come back to me. Sorry for keeping you, but I was wondering if Angelo Moretti is available today?'

'Actually, no. No, he hasn't been around for a while, he is out of the country and not to be expected back for a couple months.' Kate made something up.

'Oh.' Jen couldn't hide the disappointment.

'I could let him know that you stopped by.' Kate tried to keep the smile of relief hidden from her.

'One question: do you happen to have a picture of him?'

Kate stood there speechless, not knowing how to respond. If she said no, it could be too suspicious, she knew that she had to say yes.

'I will check for you.' With those words Kate closed the door, and right at the entrance was a picture hanging of Angelo's father. *YES.*

'Here it is.' Kate said while opening the door. Jen slowly reached for it. The man in the picture was not the man in her mind. Too hopeful, too full of disappointment. 'Oh.' Jen handed the picture back to Kate.

'Thank you for your time.' Jen turned around and slowly walked away. Kate closed the door at the same time that she let out a huge sigh of relief. She could not have Jen haunting her life. Just as she closed the door, Marcello came out of the room.

'Who was that?'

'That was someone looking for a man that doesn't live here.'

'Oh.' Marcello shrugged and went back to playing with his plane.

Discovery

Chapter Sixteen

I never told anyone that Jen had come to visit me. I couldn't have her haunt my life once again. But she did. She continued to stay in my mind, thought after thought. Conscious after conscious.

I just wanted to let it all go. Breathe it in, breathe it out. It was not until years later that I ever mentioned it to anyone, the one person that really needed to know.

She reaches out her arm and lets the light wind caress her skin, the power she feels against her fingers of air intertwines like silk falling from the sky. This is where she wanted to be, this is where she always wanted to be. A sense of belonging filled her and possessed her, yet there she stood alone, completely fulfilled with who she had become. What memories she lacked were now filled with the senses she feels with her body.

Music intrigues her ears like a memory behind her eyes. She was here before, she stood on the same ground and embraced what was before her. The music of the water, the lapping of the movement against the stone was a familiar sound. It was soothing and hopeful; she couldn't explain the logistics, but she knew the feeling and what it entailed. The sound was haunting and painful at the same time. In the wind carried the hope of taste; a scent that tickled her lips. On the island of Gudicecca where the edge of the man made land met with the bleeding waters, Jen stood looking into the Grande Canal.

The sound of a vaporetto hitting hard against the pier diverted Jen's attention to reality. The passengers took their turns getting off the boat as the others waited to step on. Today the sun decided to hide in a misty fog that lay resting low in the city's hallows.

'Madam.' The vaporetto operator took hold of her attention and signaled for her to step onto the boat. Absent minded, her feet moved from the pier to the boat. Today the maze of Venice was nothing like the maze of her mind: there was no way out.

The boat slowly motored away from the dock. She looked back as if someone was standing there to receive her stare. Someone who was saying good-bye to forever. Only that person wasn't there, that person would never be there. But at this moment there was no difference she was still saying good-bye.

The world was happening around her. If it was hectic or calm, she didn't notice. She was having her moment of complete satisfaction, complete serenity and peace. She let go of what she had been searching for her whole life. This was the first time she felt this way, she had never sat in this feeling before. Would the feeling stay? Her life had not been complete, so many things still missing, too many questions. But maybe figuring everything out wasn't what her life was about. To her, it became clear at this moment. This feeling was a victory within her mind and body. She could not hide the small smirk on her face, nor did she want to as the vaporetto left the island of Guidecca, perhaps this would be her last time. She turned to look forward. The first stop after the island of Guidecca was the San Marco piazza. A place always filled with the warmth of people. For some reason, even though she knew she was due to leave the country in a few hours, she stepped off the boat. Her mind was not telling her where to go, it was her body that led the way.

She walked into the middle of the piazza, and noted that the people were just like the pigeons flocking to a place of meeting. To go where the people go. The tower shadowed over the cathedral but the old Byzantine frescos were still present and vibrant. Today Jen couldn't stare at the wonder that was in front of her. Today the sculpting of what made up a person was just as powerful as a grand structure that still stood through the ages. And so, she stood and looked quite obviously at the people that inhabited this place. Most of who didn't know where to belong, the ones full of curiosity, so they bought a ticket and left the comforts of their homes. There was nothing else like the freedom of traveling. Jen had spent most of her life trying to know where to be. Maybe if she left somewhere she could find it, she almost forgot to create it. But she eventually did, Jen created a home like no other. A home that was made of flesh and blood a home within herself. A home that no matter where she was it came with her. And so, she belonged wherever she went.

She turned her attention to a familiar cafe and noticed a young woman sitting alone at the table. This woman belonged here, she belonged in Venice, belonged with her surrounding. She smiled, which was pronounced by the sun. Like Jen, she noticed what was around her. Once, long ago, Jen remembered that she sat there. Only for a moment, the two of them looked at each other. That woman, whoever she was, saw herself in Jen, and for that moment they looked at each other and smiled.

Jen thought about the child she had at home. A daughter who, like Jen, had wishes to become a painter. A daughter, Gabriella, who had become an artist and found the love of her life, and married the man. A daughter, who also became a mother. A daughter, who never understood her mother until the day she, too, became a mother. A woman with enough beauty to move a mountain, a woman who could seduce a man at the stare in her eyes. A woman that longed the same thing Jen once did. Where did that lead?

Laughter diverted her attention, she turned to be warded off through the glare of the sun. But beyond the first impression, there was a child, and as her eyes focused through, she saw the boy. He sat on cracked stone, playing with his plane. He smiled and reached out to her. It was that boy, almost, maybe. It was most probable that she had gone mad. But he reached for her, and Jen reached for him.

So many years ago, too many to count, and yet the boy never changed. Her imagination vividly remembered: the painting.

'Hello.', she said softly as she reached the boy, their hands almost touching.

He smiled, and laughed as she picked him up into her arms and supported the child onto her hip. She spun around as he flew his plane, the same plane in the painting. Before, Jen had continued living and sometimes she never knew why, but now she knew. This moment had come true.

'Excusi, excusi!' A voice came from behind her, a voice she recognized, a voice she never heard before. A voice that stopped her dead in her tracks. She turned slowly to face where the voice came from. In front of her stood a man, beside him the woman she had watched earlier. The couple stood there staring at her, anger morphed into compassion. Safely, Jen put the child down.

'Angelo, come here.', the woman said softly reaching for him. But the man never moved, he never diverted his attention from her.

'I'm sorry.. I thought...' Jen couldn't finish what she wanted to say. She couldn't remember what she wanted to say. 'You look like...' she laughed a little, '...you look like someone I used to know.' *Jerry.* 'I haven't seen him since high school. A long time ago.'

The man stood still. Silent. His eyes gave something away, but Jen wasn't sure what.

'Marcello, you know this woman?' the lady beside him softly spoke.

'Yes,' he looked at her a little longer: 'she is my mother.'

It was then that Jen knew: this was the moment. This moment was what she continued to live for, she waited a lifetime. She never asked how he knew her, and she never questioned if it was true or not. She knew. The world around them grew quiet. It was as though it was suctioned away from them, lost in a vortex. The sensation of her body seemed to dissipate only into emotion.

A lifetime apart had not stopped or hurt this moment in anyway. The strength between them was a force that could never be broken.

'I'm sorry,' her voice slowly came out, 'It took me forever to get here.'

Marcello's arms wrapped around Jen's body with no warning. Jen didn't want to do anything else. It was then that they both noticed each others tears.

'I have missed you.'

Jen knew that she could have died there and fulfilled that missing piece in her heart. But this moment wasn't the end, it was the beginning to a moment in her life, the moment she had been waiting for.

'How long did you know about me?' Jen asked after a long moment of silence.

'Kate always told me you would come back, but you just wouldn't know it.'

'Thank you for forgiving me, my love. Thank you.'

Once again Jen belonged to Venice, and at this moment, Venice belonged only to her. In Venice there is no regret, no wishing the past was different or life could have been easier. In Venice, it is as it is, the art of being.

-Fin-